I0760768

DEADLY WOLF BITE

MAFIA PACK #2

HEATHER HILDENBRAND

Mafia Pack, book 2

Heather Hildenbrand

Cover Design by Malice & Mayhem . Artwork by Enola Sketches

Edited by Danielle Fine. Proofread by Dawn Y

www.heatherhildenbrand.com

1

LEXI

"I won't do it," I declare, my voice wobbling only slightly.

Ramsey side-eyes me from the driver's seat of his Lykan Hypersport but doesn't respond. His face is flushed, his hair disheveled, ruining his usual laid-back, golden-boy look. Then again, considering he betrayed me to the enemy tonight, I'd say a lot more than his composure has been lost. Any trust I had for him is gone, though I can't help beating myself up for ever letting my guard down with him.

He's Grey's friend.

But I don't know him.

All I know about Ramsey Greco is that he's part of my fiancé's inner circle—and a werewolf who informs on his closest friends to the mafia pack alpha. The old me would never have trusted someone solely based on the word of another. Orphaned and mostly alone, I've survived on my wits and intuition my whole life—until being kidnapped and delivered to Indigo Hills. And now, I'm royally fucked because of this one single slip in judgment.

Ramsey sold me out, and now I'm being forced to do the same—spy on the man who kidnapped me and brought me into this mess. Shouldn't be an issue, right? Grey's more than my kidnapper, though. In a twist that undoubtedly sounds a little like mental instability on my part, he's also my best friend and someone I can't stop imagining in my future.

"I mean it," I say with more force—and less tremble—in my voice. "I won't spy on Grey for Franco. Or for you. As soon as we get back, I'm going to tell him everything."

Ramsey hits the brakes hard enough to make them squeal. My seatbelt locks as we come to an abrupt stop in the middle of the road, and a car honks as it veers around us. Bright red taillights light up the darkness until the car turns right and disappears.

I'm too shocked to say anything as Ramsey twists toward me with a vicious glare.

"You *will* find out everything you can about Grey's plans to overthrow Franco and report it all to me," he says, his tone threatening.

"Or what?" I challenge. "You'll kill me? How would you explain that to Grey? Or even Vincenzo? They'd both come for you the moment they learned what you did—no, what you *are*. A rat."

I expect a flash of temper. Maybe even violence. Instead, his lip curls with disgust. "You really don't get it, do you?" He leans closer, the leather seat crunching with his movement.

I don't move, but my body tenses at his closeness.

"Franco never wanted you here," he snarls. "That's why he left you to fend for yourself all those years. You were nothing to him. Now that you're back, you're an inconvenience at best. A complication at worst. The moment you stop serving his purposes, he will dispose of you. So if I were you, I'd start making myself useful."

"Grey would never let anything happen to me."

He scoffs. "You think Grey will believe you over me?"

I frown, suddenly less sure of myself. "I haven't done anything wrong."

He laughs harshly. "You agreed to spy. The damage is done."

"I was coerced," I remind him.

His smile is cruel and smug. "I've known Jericho Diavolo my entire life. You've known him for five fucking minutes. None of them will take your word over mine. And you've seen what we do to traitors."

I shudder as his meaning hits me. Trucker. When I first arrived in town, Grey took me to a secret warehouse to confront a pack member who'd been caught informing to Franco. Grey shot him at point-blank range right in front of me.

Yes, I know exactly what they do to traitors.

My bravery slips away with his threats, and I can't help the vulnerability that leaks into my voice. "Why are you doing this?"

Ramsey hesitates. "I don't—" He breaks off, staring out

at the road. His eyes are wild now, his breathing labored. He looks like some kind of psychotic frat boy, unhinged and single-minded in his collared shirt. "Fuck," he snarls with enough venom that I flinch.

A beat of silence passes.

His grip on the steering wheel is white-knuckled. I can't tell if he's trying to get ahold of himself or completely falling apart.

"None of your damn business," he finally snaps.

He peels his hand off the wheel and rests it on the shifter. We ease forward, accelerating slowly as we resume our drive.

My heart pounds as reality sets in.

This is happening.

If I don't betray Grey, the golden-haired devil will be my ruin.

I dart a glance at him out of the corner of my eye. His brow is twitching. His grip on the wheel hasn't eased. Whatever storm rages below the surface is still barely contained.

After a couple more turns, I recognize my surroundings. We're nearing the penthouse.

The familiar territory is a relief, even if it is my prison.

Ramsey nods at the guards then parks in the garage. We ride the elevator up in silence. I want to tell him I can make it alone from here, but after his outburst earlier, I decide it's best not to say anything at all.

When the elevator opens into the foyer, I start for my bedroom, eager to get away.

"Hey, Lexi." Ramsey's voice stops me.

I turn slowly to face him, glaring. "What?"

He walks up to me, much closer than I want him to be. His temper has cooled from earlier, his gaze sharper and more calculating. "You can do this," he says firmly.

"What if you're wrong?"

"They don't know you well enough to tell if you're lying. But they trust you. Or Grey does. He's going to tell you things he won't tell the rest of us. Well, except maybe Dutch." His expression twists with jealousy before smoothing again.

"Why not force *him* to do this then?"

"You're the weak link." His quick glance is a once-over that emphasizes his words.

"Thanks."

He scowls at my sarcasm. "You're weak without your wolf. That's just fact."

I look away, a lump forming in my throat. Up until very recently, I didn't even know werewolves existed—much less that I was descended from them. It shouldn't matter that I can't access my wolf, not when I've lived my whole life without one. But Ramsey's right. I'm surrounded by predators who've all decided I'm easy prey. If I'm going to survive a single one of them, I have to find a way to be as strong as them.

Being human in this world will only get me killed.

I have to find a way to become a wolf.

2

GREY

Dinner with Lexi was supposed to be romantic. Instead, I finish my drink and leave the restaurant exactly as I arrived—alone. My drive home is a blur of speed and reckless maneuvers. My wolf simmers at the surface, wanting to tear into something. Or someone. But Lexi's the one who ghosted me, and I could never hurt her.

Not even when she hurts me.

Ramsey's waiting in my living room when I step off the elevator. His shirt is wrinkled, and his blond hair looks as if he's been running his hand through it repeatedly. Something he only does when he's nervous or worried. My chest tightens at the sight of him—or more accurately, at the fact that there's no sign of *her*.

He starts forward. "Thanks for buzzing me in before you—"

"Where is she?" I demand.

My tone stops him in his tracks. He frowns. "In her room. Dude, she—"

I stride through the penthouse, which is dark and full of shadows, thanks to the late hour and lack of overhead lighting. The décor of this place has always been cold, but in this moment, it feels frigid. There isn't an inch of it that doesn't make me think of my asshole father. He's the one who set all this in motion. And while his scheme brought me Lexi, it also threatens to take her away from me.

Whatever made her stay away tonight, I blame him.

The man's a poison.

At Lexi's bedroom door, I don't even hesitate. Two hours of worrying and wondering and nursing my own pride have left me so twisted up that I don't even know where my fear ends and my anger begins.

I've never been stood up before, and it fucking sucks. But that's not what this is about. Lexi is mine to protect, and I can't do that if she shuts me out. A million scenarios run through my mind, each one worse than the last. We were fine this morning. A little awkward but fine. And now she can't even bring herself to eat a meal with me.

Something must've happened—but what?

My blood pumps with an anger that's a thin veneer spread over my worry. Urgency drives me to move faster.

Her door is locked, but that little detail barely slows me down. With the strength of a predator, I use my shoulder to shove it open. Wood splinters as the lock jam strips and the door swings wide.

The room is empty.

My worry spikes. I stalk to the closed bathroom door,

prepared to break it down too, but it opens suddenly, bringing me face-to-face with the most beautiful woman I've ever seen.

Lexi's green eyes go wide at the sight of me. Her white-blond hair is wet, her smooth skin clear of makeup. She's wearing a skimpy black tank top and matching pajama pants, both of which are sheer enough to leave little to the imagination. The fact that I know exactly what she looks like beneath these clothes only makes my mood more chaotic.

Fuck me, this woman has me in knots.

"Grey," she says, breathless, and my balls tighten at the way her nipples have already pebbled against her shirt. But now's not the time.

"Are you all right?" I demand, searching her for some sign of injury.

"I'm fine," she assures me.

I don't move. I'm too confused to let that be the end of it. Too wrung out not to demand answers. My father already knows she didn't show up for our dinner. He'll want answers too.

This would be so much easier if I felt some stirring of a mate bond between us, but there's nothing. The only proof I have that Lexi is my mate is that she called my wolf back to me after my father's alpha order suppressed it. Something like that could only be possible if she were my true fated mate—but there's no evidence of a bond between us, much less a wolf inside her skin. Only desire for her body and a painful twisting in my heart, an ache that's bone-deep and distracting as hell.

"Did something happen?" I ask, hating that I can't read her. "You didn't answer my calls or texts."

She ducks her head, but not before I see her cheeks flush. "I got sick."

"Sick?" I repeat, trying to wrap my head around it. "Do you need a doctor?"

"No, I think I just ate something bad at lunch. I was throwing up all afternoon."

My eyes narrow. "Ramsey said you were upset."

"I told him to say something to make you stay away."

"Why?"

"It was embarrassing. I didn't want you to see me like that."

I glance past her to the bathroom, frowning at the sight of her discarded clothes in a soaked heap in the tub. Did she throw up on them? Bleach scents the air so strongly it overpowers anything else.

"Someone should've told me. I could've at least sent you some soup or crackers."

"I wouldn't have kept it down," she says with a shudder.

My mood falters.

An upset stomach isn't a foe. With nothing to aim it at, some of my anger drains away.

"You're really all right?" I press. "Nothing else happened?"

"Like what?" she asks.

I don't want to admit to all the crazy scenarios I dreamed up out loud, so I shrug. "I don't know."

Going into it would be pointless. Besides, more than

anything, I want to find steady footing again. I want to know why things went badly this morning—to convince her to trust me again. Not easy when the reason she's here in the first place is because I kidnapped her.

"Things felt a bit awkward this morning," I say finally.

Her expression is blank for a moment before she nods. "Right. I almost forgot." At my raised brow, she adds, "A lot's happened since then."

"Can I ask you something?"

Fear flashes in her eyes before she blinks, and it's gone. "Sure."

Nerves grip me, and I have to shove the question out of my mouth before I chicken out. "Would you have come to dinner if you weren't sick?"

"What do you mean?"

"Was being sick the only reason you didn't come?"

"Yeah," she says uncertainly. "We had a deal, remember?"

A deal. Right. I agreed to help her figure out how to access her wolf if she ate dinner with me. "I see."

"Did I say something wrong?"

I shake my head. "How's your stomach now?"

"Better."

I reach out and snag a strand of her wet hair, and she flinches, so I let it fall again. She meets my gaze with something like an apology written there.

"I'm just tired," she says, the truth of her words evident in her pale cheeks and shadowed eyes.

"Get into bed," I say as gently as I can. It's not easy to

let go of the tension I've carried all evening, but I do my best. "I'm going to tell Ramsey to go."

She nods, a strange look passing over her face. "I think that's a good idea."

I press a quick kiss to her forehead and head for the living room. Ramsey's standing at the bar with a drink in hand. From the glassy look in his eyes, it isn't his first.

"Everything okay?" he asks.

"You could've told me she was sick, asshole."

He blinks then shrugs, gulping his drink.

I shake my head. "I'll talk to you later."

"You sure she's worth it?" he asks.

I pin him with a dark stare. He looks away first, and that satisfies me more than it should. "Yeah," I tell him quietly. "I'm sure."

He empties his glass then sets it aside. "See you, brother."

"Later."

He walks to the elevator and gets in. When he's gone, I engage the master lock on the keypad and arm the alarm system. We won't be disturbed again tonight.

Outside my bedroom, I hesitate. I told Lexi to get into bed, but I didn't say which one. I don't want to order her to come to me. I want her to do it willingly. To want me the way...

I shouldn't want her. Considering our families' history, I shouldn't want her at all, but we're way past what I *should* do.

Inhaling deeply, I step into my bedroom and stop at the sight of her curled beneath my sheets. She looks way too small in the large bed. Too lonely. But she's here.

She chose my room.

She chose me.

I go to her, peeling my clothes off on the way. Jacket, pants, shirt—I let them fall silently to the carpet. When I'm in nothing but my boxers, I crawl in beside her. My heart pounds with relief or pleasure, or both. Nerves grip me as I reach for her, but she doesn't pull away when I draw her against me. Instead, she cuddles closer, laying her head on my chest. Her hands are cold, so I cover them with mine. My fingers brush hers, and I look down.

"Where's your ring?" I ask.

"I took it off when I got sick."

It makes sense. The rock in that thing isn't exactly something she'd want getting dirty. And it's not like her engagement ring was supposed to be a genuine symbol of my feelings—not at first, anyway. Getting married was my father's idea. No, his order. A way to tie my family to hers. To take her birthright away from her.

She's Alpha Franco Giovanni's only living heir. Her destiny should've been to rule our pack someday, but my father will never let that happen. As the second—and lesser—alpha of this city, Vincenzo Diavolo's going to take the pack from her, one way or another. But I'm willing to bet he thinks she'll give it to him willingly.

Maybe he's right. Lexi didn't ask to be caught up in a war. And my father's not going to give her much choice. But after what he said on the phone tonight, I'm beginning to think there's more to this than a peaceful transfer of power. He said he plans to control her. He also came right out and asked if she was my mate.

I don't think he bought my lie, either.

What happens when he finds out she is?

What happens when Lexi finds out? It's bound to scare her away, and I can't afford to let that happen. I won't. It's why I don't mention that seeing her without her ring only makes me want to mark her in ways that can't be removed. Like the mark of a mate.

Her wet hair is cold on my skin, but despite the discomfort, my cock hardens at the feel of her body against mine.

I shut down the thought of getting her naked.

For now.

What she needs tonight is rest and comfort, and I intend to give her exactly that. What *I* need is for this girl to realize that none of what we're doing here is fake for me anymore. I'll do anything for Lexi Giovanni. No matter what it costs me in the end.

3

LEXI

When Grey finally falls asleep, I cling to him, trying to let the heat of his skin warm me, but nothing touches the freezing terror coursing through me. Franco's demands and Ramsey's threats hover in the forefront of my thoughts—making it impossible to think of anything else. My teeth chatter, and my heart feels like a block of ice. I've made a terrible mistake. A deadly mistake.

How could I have been so stupid?

Okay, so I'm not exactly the mafia princess they want me to be. To pretend to be. I don't know how to navigate this life, this twisted web of manipulation and deceit. I don't know how to do any of this. I should never have agreed to spy for Franco. It won't save Grey's life—because, of course, Franco will kill him when this is over anyway. Hell, I doubt it will even save mine.

Franco threw me away once without a thought. He

doesn't give a shit whether I live or die unless I can be of use to him.

And now...I can't tell Grey. There's no way he'll believe me. Not when his friend of so many years will tell him differently. Why would he put his trust in a virtual stranger over Ramsey?

You've seen what we do to traitors.

I shudder at the memory of Ramsey's words.

While Grey sleeps, I go over and over it, turning it feverishly in my mind, but I can't find an escape. Every scenario leads to death. Grey's. Mine.

Vincenzo is a world-class asshole, but at least, his plans involve keeping me alive—for now. Franco, on the other hand... The way he looked at me tonight leaves no doubt he'd kill me as soon as use me. The man might be my grandfather by blood, but he's a heartless monster as far as I'm concerned, a cruel stranger deserving of nothing but my hatred.

I still can't understand what would make Ramsey spy for that bastard. He can't possibly think Franco cares about him any more than Vincenzo does. And yet, he drove me right to Franco's doorstep and offered me up. Turned me into a traitor.

And the thought of betraying Grey... I can't bear it. He's not like his father. Not the villain I once thought he was. He's a victim of his family, just like I am. Born into this horrific game of kill or be killed.

I've only known him a short while, but already, I can't picture my life without him in it. Then again, if I don't come up with a way out for us both, neither of us will survive anyway. Star-crossed lovers, destined to be one another's downfall.

When I rub the sleep from my eyes, Grey's standing in the doorway with a tray in his hands, chasing sleep away with the scent of bacon and coffee.

"Morning," he murmurs as I sit up.

My heart flutters at the sight of him, at his tousled hair and sleepy eyes. The tattoos and cut of his jaw contradict that softness, adding to his sexiness. But as he sets the tray down on the bedside table, his expression shifts, concern clouding his features.

"How are you feeling?" he asks, his brow furrowing with worry. "Still sick?"

I shake my head, instantly tense. "I'm good."

Doubt flickers in his eyes. He studies me as if he's trying to decipher some hidden message. Guilt tugs at me, but I remain silent.

He lets it go—for now, at least—and places the tray in my lap then climbs onto the bed beside me.

"This is way too much food," I say, trying to change the subject.

"Perfect," he says. "More for me then."

We eat in comfortable silence, the only sound the clinking of cutlery against plates and the occasional sip of coffee.

But even as we share this tender moment, I can't shake

the feeling that he knows something's very wrong, that he's just waiting for me to admit it. And part of me wants to tell him, wants to confide in him and let him share the burden—to ask him to help me figure a way out of this. But another part is terrified of what might happen if I do. So, I push those thoughts aside and focus on the warmth of him beside me.

For now, that's enough.

It has to be.

When we're finished, he takes the tray and sets it aside then turns back to me, excitement sparking in his eyes. "I have a surprise for you."

Anticipation mixes with a cold dread as I try to pretend the idea of a surprise under these circumstances doesn't terrify me. "What is it?"

"Come see." He climbs out of bed and takes my hand, leading me from the room.

I half-expect us to turn for the living room where a firing squad awaits me, but he heads the other way—to my bedroom. The door hangs open at an awkward angle where he shoved through it last night. Inside, he stops and moves aside, and when I see what's waiting, I stop too.

A familiar duffel bag sits on the bed: navy blue with a small tear on the side. Whoever stuffed it full of my clothes tried to zip it shut, but the zipper hasn't worked properly in years. Beside it are two more paper shopping bags full of items. My leather bomber jacket spills out of one.

My heart swells as emotions swirl one after another.

Surprise.

Confusion.

Then gratitude and something else I can't name that leaves me warm and tingly.

I turn to Grey. "These are my things," I say, "from Lakeland."

"Yeah."

"What are they doing here?"

"I contacted the manager at the weekly motel and had him overnight everything here."

"Seriously? When?"

"Yesterday. While you were shopping with Mia."

I can only stare at him, touched that he's taken care of me—without me asking—and without a single reason to do it at all, considering the walk-in closet of clothing he's already bought me.

"Thank you," I say, my voice strangled.

Guilt weighs heavily on my shoulders. I haven't even actively betrayed him yet, and I already feel like a villain. Like a monster.

"You shouldn't have," I add, sort of wishing he hadn't. His kindness makes this so much harder.

"I want you to know that I'm sorry," he says, which has me biting back a groan. "I took you from your life, and I can't put you back. But I can bring what's left of your life to you. Or that was the idea, anyway." He looks almost sheepish.

I study him, suddenly wondering if I was wrong to assume he only wanted to take me out last night because of the paparazzi. This gesture is genuine and gains him nothing. Maybe I was wrong, and he does care…

My heart leaps at the thought.

I push up to my toes and kiss him on the cheek. "It's very thoughtful."

He grabs me and pulls my mouth against his, kissing me fervently. My guilt blooms until it's too painful to bear, but I kiss him back.

Playing the part, I tell myself. But it's more than that.

I want this.

A man who gives me unexpected gifts. Kindness. A man who takes care of me. Someone I can lean on.

It's not real. Or it won't be once he knows what I've agreed to do.

But I'm not above pretending.

From his bedroom, Grey's phone rings, and he breaks our kiss, cursing softly before doubling back to his bedroom to grab it. Alone, I look over at the bags—my bags—and listen while he speaks to whoever's calling.

"Yeah," he answers.

From his tone, I know it's not Dutch. He's too guarded for that. The only person I've heard him speak to that way is his father.

"Of course she's here," he says. "Where else would she be?"

I stiffen, unable to breathe or move while I wait for his next words. If Vincenzo's asking about me, it could mean he knows where I was last night. Who I was with. The only thing worse than Grey finding out I was with Franco is if his father does.

Grey sighs. "Fine. Where and when?"

Another pause.

Fear squeezes my chest.

His tone relaxes. "No, I'll make the reservation."

"She's fine. She got food poisoning from lunch."

He goes quiet, and I strain my ears, trying to figure out what's happe—

He's suddenly in my bedroom doorway, blocking out the light. I jump but then force myself to relax. With the phone still pressed to his ear, he's paying me no attention.

Frowning, he says, "It won't happen again."

The caller says something I can't make out, and the call ends.

"Who was that?" I ask, forcing my voice to remain even.

"My father." My legs wobble as I imagine Vincenzo discovering what I've agreed to do. "He wants us at dinner tonight."

"With him?" I ask.

"No. He doesn't want to be there. But he wants us to go somewhere public where the paparazzi can photograph us. Keeping us in the headlines as a happy couple reiterates to the public that Franco's dynasty is now merging with our bloodline. It furthers my father's attempt at a political takeover." He shrugs. "Or so he thinks."

"Why did he ask about me being sick?"

His expression clouds. "He heard about you not making it to dinner last night. He was…concerned."

"He thought I ran away."

He shakes his head, moving away to pace. "I don't

think his ego would allow that idea, but yeah, he was worried. Told me to keep you on a tighter leash."

I catch myself before protesting. That...might actually work. "Maybe you should."

He stops pacing and gives me a dubious look. I can't blame him. It's not what either of us expected me to say. But I double down on what's probably an incredibly stupid idea.

"You should," I repeat. "Keep me close, I mean. We need to show the world we're a happy couple, right? So, let's paint the picture for them. Show them what a good idea it is to merge our families."

He gives me a wary look. "We'd be giving my father what he wants."

"It's not your father people will be watching."

He doesn't respond, so I press on, latching on to the only lifeline I can think of right now. "If we can bring the people to our side, won't that help when it comes time to make your move against him? Even our odds?"

He nods slowly, though he's clearly not quite convinced. "It's true. We can't afford a pack war without bringing some of them to our side first."

"Maybe we can use these public appearances to do that." And I need to be so glued to Grey's side that I won't be able to get away long enough to give Franco any information.

It's a flimsy plan, but it's all I've got. At least until I think of something better.

"Okay." He still looks a bit unconvinced, so I smile,

hoping it comes off as genuine and not as terrified as I feel.

"What's on our agenda today? So I know how to dress."

He frowns, clearly distracted as the wheels in his head turn my words over and over. Finally, he seems to make some sort of decision.

"Wear a bathing suit," he says, "and your ring." Then he walks out, looking at his phone as he goes.

4

GREY

I dial Dutch's number, my brain kicking into gear in several directions. Lexi's idea is a good one. We'll need numbers if it comes to a war—though, hopefully, it won't. But I can't shake the feeling that there's more to it than that. She's hiding something. I just don't know what.

Dutch answers as I step into my bedroom and shut the door behind me.

"Yo," he says. "How was the big date?"

"It didn't happen."

"What?"

"She never showed."

"Shit. Is she okay? Did Franco hurt her?"

I stop cold, my gut twisting at his words. "Franco? What the fuck are you talking about?"

There's a long pause. "I'm talking about how Dom dragged her off the street and into the restaurant for some kind of conversation," he says as if this is information I should already have.

Blood pounds in my ears, my veins lacing with fury. Not just for what Franco might've done but the fact that I'm the last to fucking know about it.

"She didn't tell me," I say quietly, my body trembling as my control starts to slip. Inside, my wolf is straining to be freed, but I shove him back.

"She's probably afraid you'll do something stupid like walk in there and attack them—you know, like you already did." Dutch's attempt at a joke doesn't help, and he clearly realizes it. "Look, I got a call last night saying she was picked up. I only waited to talk to you because I figured Ramsey would've already filled you in."

The name is another jolt to my system. "Ramsey was there?"

"Yeah."

What the fuck?

"Wait. He didn't tell you either?"

I don't answer.

I can't.

My mind is going too fast and too fucking dark.

Dutch curses then goes silent. I can hear him rummaging.

"What are you doing?" I ask.

"Coming to you," he says.

"No," I say. "Don't."

"We need to talk about this."

With her.

He doesn't say it, but I know what he means. And

despite my feelings for Lexi, he's not wrong. She needs to be called out on her lie.

"I agree. But we'll do it as a group."

"You sure that's wise—putting her on the spot?"

"I'm not sure of anything except that it's time to stop fucking around and start fighting back."

"Are you saying what I think you're saying, boss?"

For once, I don't correct him or cringe when he uses that blasphemous title. "My father has his plans. We need to make some of our own."

Dutch hoots, and I feel his enthusiasm like a burning in my blood. It calls for violence. It calls for an end to the lifetime of corruption and the monsters who inflict it.

Five years ago, I thought I could fix it. When it all went to shit, I told myself leaving was the only option. But I'm done running and hiding.

"I've waited way too long to hear you say that shit," Dutch says when he stops hollering like a fucking loon.

"It's past time," I agree.

"What do you want me to tell the others?"

"We're coming to you. Call them and tell them to meet us at your place."

"You've got it. And Grey? I'm with you, man, all the way to the end."

"Thanks, Dutch. That means a lot, especially in this city."

I hang up but hesitate before going to her, debating how to handle this. She didn't tell me she spoke to Franco. She damn sure didn't tell me Dom put his hands on her.

The second thought has me vibrating with fury. But it also has my chest aching.

She doesn't trust me.

Didn't Dutch already warn me of that?

So why does it hurt when I see the evidence?

Instead of rushing back to her, I march into my bathroom, turn the shower on, and kick the shit out of the trash can. It hits the wall and bounces off before rolling across the tile. With the water turned up to scalding, I step beneath the spray and let it wash away the rest of my burning ire.

I'm mostly angry with myself, anyway.

If anyone's to blame for Lexi's secrets, it's me.

I broke things between us before I knew I wanted them whole. And I'm the only one who can put us back together. In the meantime, I plan to do everything in my power to hit Franco and Dom where it hurts. I'll make them regret coming after Lexi if it's the last thing I do.

No one touches my mate and gets away with it.

5

LEXI

Grey is quiet as we drive. Even the call from his father didn't subdue him like this. Whoever he called as he left my room earlier must've said something to piss him off, though I don't ask what. I'm not confident enough to pry. Not with the secret I'm keeping.

In the side mirror, I spot a dark car with tinted windows trailing us. Would Franco be dumb enough to put a tail on me as obvious as this one? Would Ramsey?

"Relax."

Grey's voice snaps me out of my thoughts. He lays a hand over mine. I look down and realize I've been picking at my cuticles.

"The car behind us is my security. Remember that car we took home from the engagement party?"

I dart another glance at my mirror. Sure enough, the car and driver are the ones we used for our engagement celebration a couple of days ago. My thoughts drift to what we did in that car on the way home. And in his bedroom after.

Grey's hand is warm where it rests over mine for one beat, two...

He removes it and drapes it over the e-brake instead.

I suppress a sigh and turn my attention back to the window, watching the city whir by. As we drive through downtown Indigo Hills, music streams softly through the car's speakers. I let it wash over me, enjoying the lazy, vibey acoustics after what feels like a lifetime of club beats—or "stripper ballads" as Violet called the slow songs she always selected for her stage performances.

A pang of loneliness hits me in the gut.

I don't miss my job at Shady Shag's, but I do miss Violet, my only friend. She's probably a mess from my disappearance. I don't remember much of my exit—okay, abduction—that night because I passed out from the shock of seeing Grey transform into a wolf right before my eyes, but it must seem like I vanished into thin air.

Even if I can't go back, I wish I could at least let Violet know I'm okay. The phone Grey gave me yesterday has tempted me more than once, but I can't bring myself to reach out to her with it. Tech is traceable, and I have no doubt Vincenzo would use Violet to hurt me. Could Grey's courier get her a message? The one he used to retrieve my things?

A quick glance at him makes it clear now isn't a good time to ask. His jaw is set, the muscle flexing as he grinds his teeth. He's definitely upset, which reignites my own fear.

I look away before he can see me staring.

Fidgeting again, I play with the enormous engagement ring he insisted I wear today. The diamond is heavy and blinding, not at all what I would've wanted if this engagement were real. But it's not. It's me playing a part, pretending to be someone I'm not.

And this gaudy ring symbolizes that perfectly.

"You don't like it."

My head whips up at his words. He looks from me to the ring and back again, his gaze perceptive enough that I don't bother to deny it.

"It's not what I would've chosen," I say carefully.

His mouth curves ruefully. "I guess choice wasn't exactly part of the process for either of us."

My heart pricks at that.

He didn't choose me.

Does that mean he doesn't want me after all?

"I didn't say I felt the same about the person who gave me the ring." The words are out before I can talk myself out of it.

His expression softens. For a second, he's completely open, his feelings on full display. "I hope you mean that."

His voice is rough and vulnerable, shooting an arrow of hope straight into my heart, but before I can ask if he feels the same way, his expression tightens again, and he's back to brooding.

I don't say anything else.

Twenty minutes later, we've swapped the skyscrapers

for rolling lawns that grow wider and more manicured as we wind along. Houses become larger and larger until we turn left into a gated neighborhood. Grey slows to a stop at the guardhouse and rolls his window down. But the uniformed guard merely offers a salute and waves us through without a word.

Grey waves back, and we drive on.

My worry is overtaken by awe as I drink in the beautiful houses along our route. They're set back from the road, obscured by lush trees and bright green hedges, but I glimpse enough of them to note the luxury.

After a couple of turns, Grey pulls into one of the driveways.

The sprawling mansion looks like somewhere a congressman might live. A quick count gives it at least five chimneys and four different balconies. The exterior is a cream-colored stone of some kind. And the lawn is flawless. The grass couldn't have been more perfect if someone had painted it on.

Grey parks under a covered carport on the side of the house.

"Where are we?" I ask, unable to hold in my curiosity another moment.

"Dutch's house," Grey says before climbing out.

My jaw drops as Grey rounds the car. He pulls my door open just as the security car parks behind us. I shut my mouth and climb hastily out to join him. "Seriously?"

"What? This place doesn't scream Dutch to you?"

Before I can answer, a familiar lanky figure emerges from the house. Dutch is dressed in swimming trunks and a short-sleeved white button-down left undone to reveal a surprisingly cut chest and abs.

At the sight of us, he spreads his arms wide in greeting, a bottled beer clutched in one hand. "Mi amigos," he calls as if this is some kind of reunion.

"Where are the others?" Grey asks.

"Her Majesty is out by the pool." He tips his sunglasses down his nose and glances at me. "Waiting for you," he adds. "You did bring a suit, right?"

"Under my clothes," I say, gesturing to the sundress I threw on over the blue bikini I dug out of my duffel bag earlier. It's Violet's bathing suit. She wore it for a stage performance once—some mermaid thing she decided not to do again—but it's technically a swimsuit. And despite how scant the fabric is, it makes me feel close to her to wear it now.

I need her courage today.

"Good." Dutch waves me toward the house. "Come on. I'll show you where to go while Grey and I get the snacks."

I follow them inside, trying not to gawk. Marble floors give way to buttery white furniture and matching drapes that frame large windows overlooking the backyard. I pass a gleaming sideboard and can't help but run my fingers over its pristine surface.

Grey's penthouse is nice, but this place feels like a castle.

We reach an atrium in the very center of the house, and the walkway branches in four directions. To my left, there are more rooms decorated in mostly white and an ascending staircase near a set of wide front doors. But

Dutch points to the right where French doors stand open to the outside. Beyond that, a patio beckons, and music spills in from outside speakers.

"Mia's out there," Dutch tells me.

Grey adds, "We'll be right back."

He and Dutch disappear down the hall, and I go in search of Mia, the only other woman in the friend group and one of Grey's closest confidantes. Up until yesterday, I might've considered us friends too, but after last night, I can't afford to think like that.

I find the gorgeous redhead lounging beside a pool fit for the Olympics. She wears dark sunglasses and a black-and-white striped bikini that, along with her red hair, gives off a classic-movie-star vibe. Sunlight casts her skin in a bronze glow, highlighting the freckles dotting her cheeks. The entire scene could be printed on a postcard. Only the slight breeze stirring her hair gives it away as real.

When I stop in front of her, she reaches up and slides her glasses down her nose much like Dutch did. "You're alive."

And just like that, the pretty picture is slashed into pieces, and I'm on full alert. "Was there a doubt?"

"Sit." She points to the empty lounge chair beside her.

I take it, still on edge. Does she know what Ramsey did to me last night? Does everyone? Is this a setup?

"He's not using you," she says. "Well, not entirely."

"Who?" I ask, confused.

"Grey." She says it like it's obvious, but I honestly have no idea what we're talking about here.

"Okay…"

"Look, if you don't trust him, just tell him that. You don't have to fake an illness to avoid going out with him. He's a big boy. He can handle the truth."

"I wasn't—"

Razor and Crow emerge from the house, followed by Ramsey. The three of them are laughing and hooting about something. At the sight of Mia and me, they offer boisterous greetings and matching grins.

"Fucking finally," Mia says with a huff. "You ladies take forever to answer a summons. What if it had been an emergency?"

"Crow couldn't get his hair right," Razor says, reaching out to ruffle his half-brother's hair.

"Fuck off." Crow shoves Razor.

Razor shoves him back.

They nearly knock each other to the ground in a sudden wrestling match.

"Ramsey, do something," Mia says, sitting up.

"What the hell do you want me to do?" Ramsey asks.

"Ugh. I swear, I'm surrounded by children." Mia jumps up and rushes over, easily yanking the brothers off each other. It's impressive, her tiny stature overpowering their muscular bodies. Of course, Mia's a powerful wolf shifter just like they are, but it's hard to wrap my brain around it when she's standing next to them and looking so slight in comparison.

I can't help but wish I had strength like that too.

Would Franco think twice about messing with me if I were a wolf? Would Vincenzo?

With their fight over, Mia starts lecturing the two of them about manners. I smile at their sheepish expressions—until Ramsey steps into my path, blocking my view.

My smile evaporates.

I force myself to focus on his face, bile rising. I hate the way he stands here, pretending he's not selling out his friends to their worst enemy. But mostly, I hate that he forced me to do it too—which has essentially put us on the same side. So, now the sight of him reminds me that I hate myself.

He comes toward me, his happy-go-lucky expression replaced by a tightness that hardens his sparkling blue eyes to granite. Ramsey reminded me of a Greek god the first time I saw him. Now, that's even more true, considering how fucked up and backstabbing those gods really were.

"What did you tell Grey?" he asks, pulling up a chair from the table nearby.

"About what?" I ask stubbornly.

His eyes narrow. "You know what."

I glance away from him. "I told him I was sick."

"And he believed you?"

"Yes."

He runs his hand through his hair, leaving it more disheveled than I've ever seen it. He looks ready to say more, but Mia rejoins us, followed by Razor and Crow. She drops back into her lounge chair just as Dutch and Grey appear, their arms loaded with drinks.

Dutch gives a cold beer to each of the guys while Grey hands Mia and me a can of something I don't recognize.

"What's this?" I ask.

"Hard seltzer," Mia says. "They taste way better than that crap."

"Thanks." I take it but don't open it.

Alcohol and lies don't mix well. Not for me, anyway. Ramsey, however, pops the top of his beer and swigs. The others all open their drinks, and for a moment, the small talk and laughter between them is pure friendship. The kind that can only come from a long history together.

Razor accidentally spills some of his beer on the concrete.

"Party foul," Dutch accuses.

"Chill," Razor mutters, shoving Dutch.

Dutch shoves him back, which results in Razor spilling even more beer.

"You're both heathens," Mia says.

Crow smirks at that. He catches my eye. "Don't judge us all based on my heathen brother."

"Noted," I say, returning his smile.

For half a second, I forget these people aren't my friends. Or that Crow wouldn't be this friendly if he knew where I was last night—and why. For half a second, I let myself be happy.

The illusion vanishes when I look over at Grey. He doesn't look amused like the others do. He's watching Ramsey with a deepening frown. My insides tighten, and I look away again before he can catch me staring.

"Okay," Mia says. "As fun as it is to day-drink with you assholes, can we get down to business? I have shit to do."

"You're really fucking bossy, you know that?" Dutch grumbles.

"I'm only bossy because you're all children." Mia flashes him a brilliant smile. "Someone has to be the mature one in this group."

Ramsey laughs, and Grey's gaze on him sharpens.

"Mia's right," Grey says. "We have a lot to discuss. Let's go."

Go?

Everyone moves to follow Grey, and I get the sense they've done this before. He leads them around the pool and away from the house. Ahead, the gardens spread out before us.

"Where are we going?" I fall into step with Mia at the back of the line.

She has her towel wrapped around her waist, and her dark glasses hide most of her face. In a low voice, she says, "We can't talk out in the open like this. Not with Rocco in and out of the house."

I pause, remembering the name. "Rocco is Dutch's father."

"He's the donor anyway," Dutch pipes up.

Mia looks over at me wryly. "Like I said, we can't risk him overhearing our conversations."

I nod.

Dutch's dad is one of Vincenzo's generals. In fact, every one of Grey's friends is the son or daughter of a mafia pack general. I've only met the generals once, but that was enough for me to know we don't want them to discover our plans. They're loyal to Vincenzo, and he's already proven what he'll do if Grey defies him even an inch.

We file into the pool house, which is larger and nicer than any house I've ever lived in. White carpet and beige furniture decorate the space. Artwork with relaxing beach scenes hangs on the walls. It's not quite as opulent as the main house—and a little more lived-in, now that I'm looking closer. Video games are strewn over the entertainment center's surface, and a pair of flip-flops rest upside down in the corner where someone flung them.

Dutch drops onto the couch and drapes his arm over the cushioned armrest. Razor and Crow both take a seat on the couch with him. Mia opts to stand near the window, leaning on the wall as she sips her drink.

Grey takes one of the oversized chairs opposite the couch. I take the other.

"Well?" Dutch says when everyone's settled. "What's the plan, boss?"

Grey's gaze is aimed across the room where Ramsey's standing in front of the fridge. He comes away with another beer but stops short when he sees us watching.

"What?" he asks, his golden-haired, blue-eyed look the epitome of innocence.

If I hadn't been with him at Franco's, I'd never suspect him as a traitor.

But he is.

And all I feel when I look at him is contempt.

"Before we discuss our strategy, we need to get a few things straight," Grey says. His tone is sharp, and no one says a word, even when his pause stretches.

Ramsey comes slowly forward, his drink dangling in his hand. "All right," he says warily. "What's on your mind?"

"First off," Grey says, his gaze stony, "why don't you tell me what Franco said to you last night."

Every cell in my body screams *danger.*

This is it.

He already knows—and bringing us out here to this isolated space is the perfect way to deal with us without anyone ever knowing what happened.

This isn't just a setup. It's an ambush.

Ramsey doesn't miss a beat. "Ugh, I fucking knew you'd hear about it. Listen, before you get all cocked on going after Dom, think it through."

"Of course I'd hear about it," Grey snaps. "The question is why didn't you want me to know?"

Mia shoots me a questioning glance, but I don't meet her eyes. I can't. Even without Grey's attention on me, I know he's reading my reaction right now. I'm hyper-aware of him sitting so close to me. Close enough to reach over and grab me if Ramsey decides to throw me under the bus.

The others are deadly silent, hanging on Ramsey's answer.

"Because it's not hard to figure out that you feel something for her," Ramsey says like it's the most obvious thing in the world.

Grey frowns.

I stop breathing, waiting to see how this will play out.

"And I knew the moment you heard Dom touched her,

you'd want to kill him. But listen, we can't afford that emotional shit right now, okay? Dutch, talk sense into him."

Dutch blinks, and I watch as the words click into the parts of his brain that make sense. He looks over at Grey and shrugs. "Ramsey's right. Dom deserves whatever we dish out, but we can't get reckless about it."

Grey's attention swings back to me. "Did he hurt you?" he asks quietly.

"No," I say quickly.

"The motherfucker tossed you over his shoulder, from what I heard," Dutch drawls.

Grey's eyes narrow on me.

"He did," I agree, looking only at Grey. "Dom's definitely an asshole, I'm not arguing that. But he didn't hurt me. He just wanted to scare me."

"And did he?" Grey presses. "Scare you?"

This time, I can't help glancing at Ramsey. "Yes," I say, my eyes boring into his. It's not a lie. Dom did scare me, but the damage Ramsey could do scares me more.

When I look back at Grey, his hands are fisted. He's pissed, and I can't tell how much of that temper is aimed at me.

"But Dutch is right," I add, unwilling to acknowledge that Ramsey's advice came first. "Let's be smart, not reckless."

Grey doesn't answer right away, and the fear gnaws through my control until I have to squeeze my hands together to keep them from trembling. "What did he say to you?" he asks.

"Dom?"

"And Franco."

"Franco wasn't even there," Ramsey chimes in before I can answer.

Grey rounds on him. "She can speak for herself."

Ramsey rolls his eyes like this is all just an annoyance and pops his beer open.

Grey turns back to me. His dark eyes are piercing, like he's stripping me bare. Layer by layer. Until all that exists is the truth.

"Dom wants me," I say quietly, not sure I can trust my voice any louder. "He said that…if I play my cards right, I'll get him as my prize."

Grey snarls.

"That fucker is dead," Dutch mutters.

"Yeah, but Lexi got him," Ramsey says, nodding his approval. "Gouged his face with her nails."

"Good for you," Mia says, her eyes burning so brightly I wonder if her hair will catch fire. It's the only thing she's said so far, and I swallow my guilt at lying to a girl who so obviously has my back on this.

"Anything else?" Grey asks, and I refocus on him.

"I think Dom wants me out of the way," I say because it's a thought I've had between the moments of dread over my promise to spy. "Does he stand to inherit the Giovanni pack?"

"Not officially, but the assumption was there," Grey says. "He's always strutted around like it's in the bag."

"That all went away the moment she got here," Razor says.

The others frown.

I search their faces, hungry to understand more of this world to help me survive it. "Is that how it works?" I ask. "Franco could name another heir instead of me, and they'd just get everything?"

"Not with you alive and in this city," Dutch says pointedly.

I try not to think about the alternative to either of those things.

"So, right now, if I'm…here, and something happens to Franco, I inherit his title?" I ask.

"Traditionally, you would, yes," Grey says, "But…"

"But?" I prompt.

"You're not bound to anyone yet," Mia says when no one else speaks up. "It's archaic and sexist as fuck, but until you and Grey are married, you're fair game for claiming. Dom could use that. Force you to marry him instead. Then he'd kill you and get your title."

I shudder at the casual way she tosses out the idea of my death. "Why bother to marry me before killing me?"

"Because you're not a wolf," Dutch says.

I frown. "So, if I were a wolf, he'd just kill me."

Dutch shrugs. "Probably."

Mia reaches over and smacks the back of his head.

"Ow," he says. "What?"

She sighs. "Since you're human, Dom would need a legal tie to you. Otherwise, anyone could challenge his rule as alpha if you were out of the picture," she says. "Not to mention, Dom would have to fight any challenger, and the coward doesn't want to do that."

"So, as a single, unmarried human, I'd have a better chance of keeping my title," I say, trying to wrap my head around all the technicalities.

"It's hard to say," she admits. "We've never had a human alpha before. Normally, if you kill an alpha wolf, you inherit their title and power. But since you're human, there's no power to inherit. Only the title. Keeping it might be harder."

"I don't know. The generals would probably accept her," Dutch says. "Or Santiago and Conrad would, at least. She's Franco's bloodline, which would carry a lot of weight with them. But also, no offense, Lexi, they'd see you as someone to manipulate for their own gain."

"True," Mia says. "They'd probably just suck up to convince you to relinquish the title to them instead. Or give them more power than they had before."

"So why doesn't Franco just name Dom and be done with it already?" I still can't figure out why Franco hasn't disowned me—or killed me—if he hates me so much.

"That's a great question," Dutch drawls.

I glance from him to Grey as the two share a look I can't decipher. My body's still wound tight from the questions, and something tells me I'm not out of the woods yet.

"Franco's playing a game of his own," Mia says thoughtfully. "He doesn't do anything without good reason."

"We can't underestimate him," Dutch says almost reluctantly. "He's remained in power this long because he's smart."

I study Grey, looking for any sign he's on to me.

"If anyone wants out, now's the time to say so," Grey adds. "Because if we're discovered by either side, or if we fail, there'll be no escape. Not like last time." He winces as he adds, "I won't be able to take the heat alone again."

"Bro," Dutch says earnestly, "we don't want you to. That's what I've been saying since you left. I'm with you until the end, no matter what happens. And I don't want you taking any more of my punishments, do you hear me?"

Razor and Crow both offer their agreements.

I think of the way Vincenzo punished Grey just a few short days ago—extra hits because he insisted on taking everyone's share on himself. It was one of the hardest things I've ever had to watch. The fact that it wasn't the first time he's done it for them touches my heart and inspires a loyalty no one else ever has.

Ramsey catches my eye, and as if he can read my thoughts, his mouth presses into a hard line, and his eyes flash a warning.

I meet his gaze defiantly, refusing to be cowed.

Mia pushes off from the wall, straightening to her full height, which isn't much, but she manages to make it look both regal and terrifying. "You know how I feel, but I'll say it again if you need to hear it. Those two asshole alphas need to be removed, and I'll sleep even better knowing I'm the one who took them out. I agree with Dutch. I can take my own lashes from now on."

Grey grunts. I can tell he doesn't like the idea of letting

them take a beating, but he nods then finally turns to Ramsey.

"Bro, I would take the alpha's wrath for us both, you know that," Ramsey says, and I swallow the acid that burns my tongue.

The fucking liar.

Grey is somber as he nods in appreciation, and my entire body fills with revulsion. I do my best to keep my fury buried far beneath the surface of my skin, but I also make myself a promise. No matter what it takes, I will find a way to stop Ramsey Greco from harming these people.

"I agree with the others," I say resolutely enough that all eyes suddenly turn to me, including Grey's. "If it comes down to it, let me take my own punishment."

"Lexi," Grey begins. "You're not exactly strong like the rest of us—"

"Don't patronize me," I cut in, furious that he's right. "And don't treat me like I'm less than them just because I don't have a wolf," I add, gesturing to the others. "If I'm in this, I'm one of you. An equal. Which means I get to say what happens to me. I get to choose the danger I put myself in. And if I get caught, I'll accept the consequences of those decisions. Not you."

Grey's gaze is a thousand pounds heavier than it was a moment ago, but there's no suspicion, only regret. Finally, he nods, his shoulders sagging even though we all just pledged to die for our cause if necessary. Or maybe that's what he was hoping to avoid when he fought against taking on this war in the first place.

"All right," he says finally. "We're all in this, equal shares."

There's a collective exhale. And I realize the others were worried he wouldn't agree to this. Suddenly, Grey's decision feels like a big step for this group. One they've been waiting for a lot longer than I've been here.

"This war won't be easy." Grey sounds tired. Like he's seen the future and is already exhausted by it. "We're going up against two powerful alphas. Neither of which has ever been even remotely threatened by anyone who tried to take them down, which means it'll take all of us working together if we're going to beat them." He pauses then adds, "Like a pack."

Dutch's eyes go wide. "Are you saying what I think you're saying?"

Grey glances at Ramsey then back at Dutch as he nods. "I think so. I've been feeling it for a few days now."

The others all exchange glances.

"Seriously? When?" Razor asks.

I listen intently, trying like hell to figure out what they're talking about.

"I think it started when we met at the lake house," Grey says. "We made an agreement as a group, and something changed."

"I don't fucking believe it," Dutch says with wonder shining in his gaze.

He looks at Mia, who grins. "Fucking finally."

"Holy shit," Razor mutters.

Ramsey and Crow both look stunned.

"Sorry, um, what exactly are we talking about here?" I finally ask.

"Grey's an alpha," Mia declares.

"Sshh," Razor shushes her.

"What? No one can hear us," she says, her joy undimmed.

"*Becoming* an alpha," Grey corrects.

I look back at Grey, trying to understand the implications of this development. "You're an alpha…like Vincenzo?"

"Not quite," he says. "My wolf's still transitioning, so I don't have the same level of power. Besides, hopefully, I'll never be an alpha like him."

"Right, sorry," I mumble. "I just… Is this common?"

"No," Dutch says, grinning like he just won the lottery. "It's been a long fucking time since this city had another alpha in it." Then his expression clouds. "Wait, do you think the others can sense you?"

Grey shakes his head. "No, I can barely sense it myself. Look, it's not something we can use in our favor—yet. I need time. *We* need time—to bond."

"Right. We should do a pack run." Razor nudges Crow. "Isn't this crazy? A pack run with just us."

Crow leans forward, clearly interested. I ignore the pang in my gut at knowing I'll be left out.

Grey nods. "We'd have to find a way to do it without the alphas knowing."

"We could really use a hex blade right about now," Razor grumbles.

"We wouldn't need to do a run if we had one of those," Crow says wistfully.

The others murmur in agreement.

"What's a hex blade?" I ask.

"It's a magical blade that binds souls through a loyalty pledge and blood magic," Mia explains. "It makes your pack bond stronger and, therefore, makes the alpha's power stronger."

"It also roots out anyone disloyal," Dutch says. "Compels them to tell the truth. Finding Trucker would've been a hell of a lot easier with one of those."

His words stab fear into my gut. "Does Franco or Vincenzo have a hex blade?"

"Franco outlawed them," Crow says. "He realized it would be too easy for others to gain power with the help of a blade. And he couldn't have that kind of threat to his position. Anyone found with one is executed."

Horror and relief swirl in equal parts inside me.

Ramsey smirks, clearly better than me at pretending a hex blade wouldn't be his absolute ruin. "He only outlawed them when his got snatched. Sore loser, if you ask me."

"Snatched by who?" I ask.

"They say the hexerei came and took it back when they saw Franco's corruption," Mia says. "Anyway, now the alphas have to rely on sheer numbers rather than the strength of a loyalty pledge. But it's not as strong as a soul binding with a hex blade."

"Even if we had one, my wolf isn't ready for that yet," Grey says. "The alpha change doesn't happen overnight. In the meantime, we still need to work our plan from all angles."

"Hell yeah." Razor hits his fist against his open palm. "Where do we start?"

"For now, we do this slow and methodical," Grey says, shaking his head to cut off whatever violence Razor's about to propose.

"Slow and methodical?" Razor repeats. "What the hell does that mean?"

"This war won't be won with violence. Not entirely," Grey says, and Razor closes his mouth with a huff. "These days, blood is drawn with words as much as weapons."

"You want to fight politically," Mia says, a gleam in her eye.

Grey nods. "For starters. We need to win public favor to our side."

"That sounds boring as fuck," Ramsey complains.

I roll my eyes. He probably means it won't make for juicy intel when he runs back to Franco.

"Yeah, I want to smash heads," Razor adds.

Dutch leans forward, ignoring them. "Your dad and Franco have fought politically for decades, boss. How do you plan to do it better?"

"Politics is about popularity," Mia chimes in. She smiles like she already sees the finish line. "It's just like high school. We start by getting ourselves crowned prom queen."

"Prom queen?" Razor's brows crinkle. "What the fuck? When did we decide to go to prom?"

"It's an expression, you asshat," Crow mutters.

"Oh." Razor looks like he still doesn't get it.

"We earn the favor of the people," Dutch says. "Get the public on our side so those assholes are left out in the cold when it all goes down."

Grey nods. "That's where we'll start. This is a long game, not a smash and dash like we're used to." He throws a look at Razor, who huffs.

"We need to know Vincenzo's plans too," Mia says. "We can't afford any surprises from him."

Grey nods. "Let's use the access we do have to our fathers to find out what we can."

"Grey's right, boys," Dutch says. "We're playing chess, not checkers. At least until our fearless leader here is strong enough to challenge Vincenzo for alpha. After that, it's check-fucking-mate for Franco."

"Correct me if I'm wrong," I say. "But winning the public over seems like an easy task. Neither Vincenzo nor Franco is particularly likable. And Vincenzo's already ordered me and Grey to use our date tonight to schmooze the media."

"Exactly," Mia says almost gleefully. "Vincenzo will think we're following his orders until...*boom*. We'll turn all those people to our side. He'll have to watch his people become our people—right under his nose. By the time he realizes our pack is bigger than his, it'll be too late."

Grey nods, his eyes glittering with the promise of the future he's painted. "As long as we stick together, nothing can stop us."

I swallow hard, trying not to think about what will happen to Grey when it all falls apart.

6

GREY

Dressed in a shirt and tie, I pace in front of the windows of my apartment, my thoughts consumed by the woman in the back bedroom—and the secrets she's keeping. Since the moment I confronted her at Dutch's earlier, her anxiety's been through the roof. It's more than her pounding pulse and jumpy movements. Her fear permeates the air between us. My sensory awareness of her emotions is more proof.

She's my mate.

And she's lying to my face.

It's not just her either. Thanks to my growing alpha power, my wolf tasted the lie in his words the moment Ramsey spoke today.

The question is what the fuck to do about it.

From the direction of Lexi's bedroom, a blow dryer begins running. We still have plenty of time before our dinner reservation, so I dial Dutch.

He picks up quickly, but the music in the background nearly drowns him out.

"Yo," I barely hear him say. "Hang on." A second later, the music shuts off. "What's up?"

"They're hiding something about last night."

"Yeah," he says on a heavy sigh. "I had the same feeling."

"Fuck."

Lexi's secrecy at least makes sense. She doesn't know me. Hasn't yet learned to fully trust me. But Ramsey? He's supposed to be one of the few I can always count on. Clearly, he doesn't feel the same about me. Not anymore. Maybe Lexi's not the only one whose trust I need to earn.

"You want me to talk to him?" Dutch asks.

"Nothing that direct," I say.

"Tail?"

I hesitate, considering the idea. If Ramsey lied because he doesn't trust me, it won't help for him to discover one of us is following him. But I need to be sure there isn't something more to it. "Put Crow on it. He's the most discreet."

"You could just compel Ram to tell you the truth," he says.

I scowl. "I'm not strong enough. Not yet."

"Damn. What about her?"

I look down the hall toward Lexi's closed bedroom door. Even with the mate bond coming to life, I can't read her feelings for me, thanks to the distance she keeps between us. It grates on me. Makes me doubt myself in a way I never have before. And I can't afford doubt—not now. Not when we're going to war. Not when I could so easily lose her.

The fact that she didn't tell me what happened last night speaks volumes about her faith in me right now.

"I need her to trust me—on her own terms," I say finally.

"I don't disagree, but time is of the essence here."

"I know."

He pauses then says, "You could just claim her. Even without her wolf, you'd read the truth from her."

"I won't force her," I growl, my temper lashing out, hot and aggressive.

"Whoa, okay. Chill, dude." He sighs. "I mean, you could ask her permission first."

"And what if it doesn't work?" I demand, my voice rising.

"She's stronger than you think. She'd be fine."

I don't bother to argue something so non-negotiable. Instead, I change the subject. "Did you learn anything about my father's comment? About controlling Lexi or about why she can't access her wolf?"

"It's been less than a day since you asked, dude." When I don't respond, he adds, "So, no. I haven't learned anything."

"Time is of the essence here." I toss his words back at him, impatience fueling my temper.

"Very funny. Dude, relax. We'll figure it out. I'm sure he just meant that he could use alpha compulsion on her once she's turned," Dutch says.

In the background, something echoes as it falls over

and rolls away. I shake my head, picturing the mess of empty beer cans and chip bags that's Dutch's private suite. The entire Marini estate is immaculate thanks to the housekeeping services Sonesta employs, but Dutch refuses to allow them into his space. And it shows.

"Maybe," I allow. "But the asshole always has something else up his sleeve."

"Like what?"

"That's what we need to find out. Has your old man said anything?" I ask.

"Only that Lexi's the key to finally wiping the Giovanni bloodline from this city for good—and other dramatic, war-criminal shit like that."

I sigh. Rocco still doesn't fully trust Dutch, and while his hesitance is clearly for good reason, it's slowing us down. "See what you can find out about why Lexi's parents left town in the first place. It might give us a clue or direction to look in for what happened to stifle her wolf."

"I'm on it," he says, and I picture him sitting down in front of his computer.

He's not the best hacker we have access to, but he's the most determined. And the most loyal. After today, I'm keeping my circle of trust small.

"Call me when you've got something."

I hang up as the blow dryer shuts off. It's not like Lexi's human ears could've heard me anyway, but I'm not taking chances. Not with whatever secrets she's keeping.

A moment later, Lexi's door opens. The click of the

latch is a little off, thanks to my rushed repair job earlier, but it's better than it was before.

I slide my phone into my pocket as she emerges from the hall. My heart skips a beat and my cock twitches at the sight of her.

The red dress she's chosen has a plunging neckline that fuels my imagination and makes it hard to look her in the eye. The softness of the fabric as it clings to her skin makes me want to run my hands over it—over her. She's piled her white-blond hair high on her head, leaving her throat bare, and my wolf stirs, telling me to mark her and be done with it.

"You look amazing," I rasp.

She brightens at my compliment, but nerves are dancing in her gaze. "Is it okay?" she asks, smoothing the nonexistent wrinkles.

I take her hand and kiss it. She's wearing the ring I gave her, and it pleases me more than I let on that, at least for tonight, everyone will see that she's mine. "It's fucking perfect."

We take the car and driver, mostly so I can stare at Lexi unhindered but also because the added security is necessary for tonight's adventure. On the way over, I try to prepare her for the circus that awaits us, though I'm pretty sure words can't convey the overwhelm of being the focus of hungry paparazzi in this city.

"They're going to ask you questions," I tell her, angling my body so that we face each other on the bench seat.

"Should I answer?" she asks.

"If you want to. Just know that anything you say will

be printed and blogged and blasted into the ether for eternal posterity." I catch myself staring, distracted by how gorgeous she looks tonight.

Her smile is rueful though a little forced. "In other words, your father and my grandfather will hear about it."

I blink, trying to refocus. "Exactly."

"Which means I should answer some of them—strategically, of course."

"That might be smart," I agree, proud of her for catching on to this fucked-up game so quickly.

"We want them to like me," she says, but it comes out like a question, and I sense her nerves returning.

I take her hand again, turning it over and smoothing her palm with my thumb. "We want them to like *us*," I correct. "They're going to love *you*, no question."

She looks reassured for a moment, but then the car pulls to a stop in front of the venue, and the cameras begin flashing. Even through the tinted glass of the back window, it annoys me. Growing up on display wasn't easy, but having to put the woman I love through it is so much worse. The fact that it's necessary only makes me angry at myself.

Lexi looks at them with trepidation but doesn't flinch. "I guess that's our cue."

I climb out of the car first, reaching back for Lexi. Her grip is firm as I lead her through the small crowd already waiting for us outside the restaurant. Security is doubled tonight, and my father's men press in close, creating a protective wall. Reporters snap pictures at an alarming speed as I push past as gently as I can. They also toss questions at us rapid-fire.

"What designer are you wearing?"

"What do you think of Indigo Hills?"

"Will you live in the penthouse or at Franco's once you're married?"

Most of them are easy to ignore.

"Who has a worse temper—Vincenzo or you?"

That one is aimed at me, but I don't acknowledge it.

"What does Vincenzo think of your work history?"

That one's clearly for Lexi, but she doesn't respond. I bite back the urge to shove the asshole who said it. This game relies on both of us keeping our cool.

Don't be reckless.

"Have you decided on a location for the ceremony yet?"

"What does Franco say about your engagement?"

"Are you and your grandfather close?"

Lexi pauses at that last one. She meets my eyes, and a slow but sure smile spreads across her gorgeous face. She turns to the journalist who asked her the question and gushes, "My grandfather and I are overjoyed at being reunited. We're getting to know one another slowly, amid wedding planning, of course. I'm just so thrilled to have gained two new families." She puts her other hand on my arm and squeezes affectionately.

The crowd gives a collective "aww," and just like that, she's won them over.

"And what about you, Jericho?" the journalist asks.

"You were gone for so long. How is it to be back home after all this time?"

He's used my real name, reminding me of who I was before I left. It grates on me, but I hold my composure.

The crowd is silent, waiting.

"I've missed it," I tell them, surprised to realize I mean it. I love this city. Aside from my asshole father and that prick Franco, anyway. Maybe that's what prompts me to keep going. "Indigo Hills will always be home, but now I get to share it with someone who means the world to me. We're looking forward to putting roots down here. Together."

Lexi's smile is sweet as she looks back at me. The crowd sighs and snaps more photos. Before they can ask anything else, I wrap my arm around Lexi's waist and whisk her inside.

The maître d' escorts us to our table without so much as asking my name. I'm used to it, the recognition, but I don't miss the way Lexi's brows lift.

At the table, a woman rises to greet us. And even though she's a welcome sight, I stiffen for a moment at her unexpected presence. Lexi does the same, though her polite expression never wavers.

"Surprise," my mother says with a genuine smile. She stands to greet us, sparkling in a silver gown, and gestures to the two empty chairs across from her. "I'm sorry. I hope I'm not intruding," she adds. "If I am, please tell me to go."

"Of course not," I say, glad for the distraction. Not just for me but for Lexi too.

Every patron in the place is watching us, and reporters

are already standing at the window and snapping pictures through the tempered glass. It's mildly annoying, but nothing I can't block out for the duration. Lexi isn't so practiced, and her gaze is drawn that way over and over again.

"We're happy to see you, Mom." I lean in to press a kiss to her cheek.

"Are you sure?" My mother turns to Lexi. "Vincenzo mentioned you'd be here, so I decided to surprise you. But if you'd rather be alone, I can go."

"No, please, Mrs. Diavolo," Lexi says, gesturing to the chair my mother rose from. "Join us. We did promise you a dinner."

"Yes, you did," Mom agrees warmly. "And call me Serena."

We all take our seats. I tuck in close beside Lexi, fighting the urge to run my hand over her thigh beneath the table.

"I ordered us some wine," Mom says as the waiter appears and pours for us. "I figured you both might need it after running that gauntlet."

"I'm grateful." Lexi picks up her wine glass. "It was quite an entrance."

"You looked like you handled it well," Mom tells her.

Lexi's cheeks flush a little at the compliment. "Thanks. I tried to give them enough information to take the edge off."

Mom laughs. "A pro already."

"I don't know how you guys live like this all the time," Lexi says, her gaze darting toward the window again.

"You get used to it," Mom says, but I know better. She hates it as much as Lexi does, which is why she spends most of her time at the lake house where the distance keeps the vultures away. Not to mention my father.

"I hope not," Lexi says. "I think that might mean I don't value my privacy as much as their flattery."

My mother gives Lexi an appreciative look. Then, to me, she says, "This one has her head on straight."

"She does," I agree. "I hate to ruin that about her."

"Nonsense. She has you to help her navigate. She'll be fine."

Her words are meant to reassure me, but they also make me feel guilty. Mom should have someone too. But my father's never been a source of protection or support. She's gotten through this life all by herself.

"Now, what fun things have you been able to do so far?" Mom asks.

"Um..." Lexi hesitates.

"We haven't exactly had time for fun, Mom."

"That's unacceptable," my mother says. "You could at least show her that this city has some redeeming qualities." She launches into a list of places Lexi should visit.

I remain silent, watching, listening, reading between the lines of Lexi's body language, and tuning into the conversations happening around us. I'm not overly worried about an ambush from Franco, but Dom's behavior last night—grabbing her off the street if their story is to be believed—means I can't afford to let my guard down anywhere. As instructed, my security team is seated at the bar to keep an eye out, but I know better than to rely entirely on their protection.

If I'm going to earn loyalty and build a pack, it'd be smart to start with the men hired to protect us. But I'll need to be careful, not showing my hand unless I'm sure they won't go running to my father.

After dinner, Mom turns the conversation to Lexi's life. "And what hobbies were you interested in?" she asks. "Theater? Sports? Grey played lacrosse in high school, which didn't leave much time for anything else."

Lexi hesitates. "Um, no theater for me."

"Sports then?"

Lexi's gaze shifts away. "No."

"Academics? Scholastic clubs? Debate?"

She smiles, but it's more of a grimace. "Nope."

My mother's forehead crinkles in confusion. "Did your adopted parents not encourage you to try things?"

"I grew up in foster care. Group homes, mostly. There wasn't much chance for extracurriculars."

Mom's expression fills with sympathy. "Oh, I didn't realize. I'm sorry. That must've been hard."

"It's not your fault." Lexi's knee bounces under the table.

Mom reaches over and pats Lexi's hand. "Maybe not, but just in case those responsible haven't apologized, someone needs to."

"Thanks." Lexi flashes a tight smile.

I squeeze her thigh. She jumps, but when I move to take my hand away, she grabs it, holding it in place. My entire body recalibrates toward her touch.

"I mean it, Lexi," Mom goes on. "Your mother was a beautiful soul. What happened to her—to you all—is a tragedy I deeply regret."

Lexi's hand tightens on mine. "You knew my mother?"

Both of us look at my mother with renewed intensity.

Mom's smile softens, and her gaze draws inward to some memory. "Cari and I were both outsiders who found ourselves suddenly on the inside. Trust was difficult, but we shared a sense of camaraderie over that, at least."

"What was she like?" Lexi says, clearly hanging on every word.

"A revolutionary," my mother declares with a wistful smile. "She wanted to change things, to really make a difference for the people in this city." Her smile fades, and a shadow overtakes her features. "When she and Monte left, everyone was so shocked by it, but I wasn't."

"Did she tell you where they were going?"

"No. But I think Cari realized at a certain point that the only thing changing was her. This world sucks you in and spits you out. She saw the inevitability of that, I think, and did the only thing she could."

"She saved herself," Lexi murmurs.

Mom reaches across the table and squeezes Lexi's hand. "No, darling. She saved you."

Lexi is quiet for the rest of dinner.

Afterward, Mom walks us out, and while she waits for her driver to pull around, she hugs Lexi in front of the paparazzi. Her smile is brilliant and affectionate as she cups Lexi's cheeks in her hands.

"I am so sorry," she whispers. "For all of it. Be strong. And come to me if you ever need anything."

"I will," Lexi tells her.

When it's my turn, I hug my mother and kiss her cheek. "Thank you."

Her response is a single word that's more like a plea. If I wasn't sure before whether my mother suspects my true intentions, her message makes it clear. And I feel the desperation and conviction of it all the way into my bones. "Win."

7

LEXI

After the cacophony of probing voices and dozens of flashing cameras aimed at us all evening, returning to the privacy and quiet of the apartment is a welcome reprieve. I played the game—for better or worse—but it's not a role I'll ever enjoy.

"My mother likes you," Grey comments before I can escape to my room.

I turn back, hating how his words make me feel.

His mother's approval leaves a sour taste in my mouth and only adds to the heavy mantle of guilt on my shoulders. She seems pure-hearted in a way that highlights my treachery. That he seems so pleased by her approval makes it all the more shameful.

He doesn't deserve what they're making me do.

Neither does she.

"She's very sweet," I say because it's the only response that isn't another lie.

"She's had it pretty rough," he says, his gaze darkening. I suspect that's putting it mildly considering she's married to Vincenzo. My heart aches for what that must be like.

"The stuff she said about my mom," I can't help but ask, "Do you think it's true?"

"My mother wouldn't lie to you." He takes a step closer to me, and I tense. If he tries to touch me, I'm not sure I can keep my armor up. "I promised to help you find your wolf. And I think that starts with learning more about your parents."

I perk up at that. "You're going to help me?"

"We had a deal, remember? You have dinner with me in exchange for me helping you."

"Right."

It was supposed to be a different dinner. A private one. But he doesn't point out that I broke that deal when I didn't show up last night.

"What are you thinking?" I ask.

"If your parents decided to leave, they would've had a plan."

I've been thinking the same thing. "Someone on the outside."

He nods. "If we could track that person down, they might be able to tell us what happened to your wolf."

"That was two decades ago. How in the world would we find them?"

"We can start with the car they were found in," he says, and I swallow hard, remembering how it felt when I learned that the story I'd been told my whole life was a lie.

Social Services said it was a car accident, but when I was eighteen, I found a single scrawled note in my social worker's personal file on me that revealed they'd both died from a gunshot wound to the chest.

"The police report had a license plate," I say.

He nods. "There's no guarantee the car wasn't stolen, but I'm having Dutch look into it." He frowns, which dampens my hope.

"What is it?" I ask nervously.

"Just something my father said," he says distractedly. His phone rings, cutting off any further questions. He checks it and scowls. "Speak of the devil. Hello?"

He listens for a moment, and I watch his expression for some clue about what Vincenzo might be saying to him. But Grey's darkening mood is no different than any other encounter he's had with the alpha so far.

A moment later, he holds the phone out to me. "He wants to talk to you."

I hesitate but then realize refusing will only force him to come here in person.

I take the phone. "Hello?"

"You can't feel your wolf at all?"

I look at Grey, bewildered, but he just shrugs. "Excuse me?"

"Your wolf," he says, impatience lacing the words. "You can't feel it even a little bit?"

"No."

"And you had no idea about being a shifter before coming here?"

"No. Why?"

"Do you ever get sick?"

My confusion turns to suspicion. "Why are you asking me—"

"Answer the fucking question."

I sigh. "I guess. Doesn't everyone?"

"When was the last time?"

I hesitate, trying to think back. "I can't remember." He snarls, and I hurry to add, "My social worker said there was something in my file. I got a high fever as a baby, and the doctors were worried because no antibiotics worked at first. Why?"

"That was the only time?"

"I think so."

He grunts like I said something helpful. "Give the phone back to Jericho."

I do as he asks, glad to be done with the sudden interrogation but mystified by what it all means. Grey listens to whatever Vincenzo's saying, his expression no help in deciphering the answers to my questions.

Lost in thought, I walk to the kitchen and help myself to a glass of water. When I turn back, Grey's still standing where I left him. He's hung up, and his expression is a bit stunned.

"What did he say?" I ask quickly.

"He said...good job."

"What did you do?"

"Not me. You."

"What did I do?" I ask warily because earning the

asshole's approval makes me almost as nervous as provoking his ire.

"The interview you gave to the paparazzi. The comments about Franco and you being one big happy family. He loved it. Said it was a nail in the old buzzard's coffin. He wants us to keep talking to the press like that. Use our comments to paint Franco into a corner."

"I mean, that was our goal anyway," I say with a shrug.

"It was. It's just weird to have his appreciation."

"It won't last," I warn.

He shakes himself, his gaze sharpening. "No, but it makes playing our games that much easier if he thinks we're playing his."

He walks over and wraps his arm around my waist, pulling me close. If he notices me stiffen, he ignores it, tucking my hair behind my ear.

"You're so beautiful," he says, brushing my lips with a kiss.

I try to keep my body and brain separate as he deepens the kiss, his arms around me tightening in a possessive hold. But it's impossible not to respond to the way he touches me. The way my body wants him to. Impossible to ignore the way my heart fills and stutters.

"You've been distant," he says when he finally eases back. "Are you okay?"

"I'm fine," I say, my voice raspy with desire. "Tonight was a lot. With the press and the paparazzi."

"Mmm. You would tell me," he says a bit more sharply, "if there was something else?"

My heart races. "Like what?"

I brace myself, but instead of answering outright, he says, "I've never introduced my mother to anyone before."

"Really? She doesn't know Dutch or Mia?" I tease.

He smirks. "Sure, but I'm not taking them home and doing this to them afterward."

"I wouldn't mind seeing you try it with Razor," I joke.

He flashes a grin as he runs a hand up my thigh and along the edge of my panties.

I draw in a sharp breath as anticipation builds.

"Grey," I manage, my emotions swirling with the need for this to be real. No pretending. No more lies between us than the one I'm already being forced to live. "Do you mean this?" I whisper as he trails kisses down my throat.

He pulls away, and I feel suddenly lonely without his hands and mouth on me. "You think I would do this with you if I didn't mean it?"

"I don't know."

His expression flashes with irritation, but then he calms and says, "Give me your hand."

Tentatively, I place my hand in his. He grips it firmly and uses his other hand to pull the giant engagement ring off my finger.

"What are you doing?" I ask, terrified he's changing his mind.

Maybe even pretending is too much.

"This ring was chosen by someone on my father's payroll. It's a symbol of the evil that brought you here. It's all wrong." He hesitates, his gaze scanning the kitchen behind me. "Come here."

With my hand still firmly in his, he leads me into the kitchen and pulls open a drawer. He rummages and comes away with a twist tie. Then he wraps it around my finger, twisting it until it's formed a ring.

"What is this?" I ask.

"It's real," he says simply. Then he drops the engagement ring back into my hand. It feels heavy on my palm. "And it's your choice. You can wear the twist tie, which is something I chose without being ordered to do so and a symbol of my feelings for you. Or you can wear this gaudy diamond my father bought."

My heart flutters then races. "Your feelings for me..."

"Are real as fuck, Lexi." His voice dips earnestly low, and he steps closer, his eyes fastened intently on mine. "That dinner the other night—when you got sick? It was my way of showing you that you matter to me. You're the most important thing in my life now."

My heart melts into a pool of warmth. "I thought it was a chance for the paparazzi to see us together."

He shakes his head. "No one asked me to take you to dinner. It was all me."

"I didn't realize..." A lump forms in my throat as I imagine him sitting at the table alone, waiting for me—while I was busy agreeing to betray him.

Guilt slams into me.

As much as I wanted this declaration from him, it only makes things harder now.

I look away, but not before he frowns at the pain I must've let show.

He grimaces, misreading it. "Fuck. It's too fast, isn't it?"

I start to answer, but he shakes his head, cutting me off as he grips my arms. "I know the situation is fucked up. And that I have to earn your trust. But dammit, Lexi. I want you. Tell me how to earn you. What can I do?"

It's not a question I'm expecting, and for a moment, I'm at a loss. He's made it clear I'm more than just a convenient distraction or a means to an end in this war with his father. But letting myself believe him is terrifying. If he's serious, it makes my betrayal so much worse.

I'm not just betraying him; I'm betraying myself.

Because the truth is I want to earn him too.

"Earning trust isn't something you do just once," I say, hating myself a little more with every word. "Especially when this world and the people we're up against are constantly chipping away at it."

"I get that," he says. "Believe me. I'm very aware that the only reason you're here is because I'm forcing you."

"It's not the only reason," I say softly.

Hope blooms in his dark expression. "It's not?"

"I told you I'm part of this now. Willingly. We made a deal, remember?" My smile is crooked.

"Yes," he says. "I can't forget. You made me promise to help you go home when we're finished here."

"You make it sound like you didn't want to agree," I say, trying to make it a joke.

"I was willing to do what you wanted—to make you happy," he says quietly. "But no, I don't want to give you up."

Fear and hope send my heart tripping over itself. I bite my lip. "You want me to stay?"

"I do," he says quietly.

No hesitation.

No wavering.

It guts me. Maybe that's why I decide to tell at least one truth. "I want that too."

8

GREY

I brush my fingers across the twist tie I've wrapped around Lexi's ring finger. The idea of her staying in this city—staying with me—changes everything. Even as my heart expands at her words, my muscles tense at the risk.

"You should know it will be dangerous," I warn, the need to protect eclipsing everything else as I imagine our lives together in a place like Indigo Hills. "Living here… there will always be enemies who would try to challenge us."

"You act like my old life was all sunshine and rainbows," she jokes, but the shadows in her eyes remind me it's not funny. Lexi's never had it easy. Her smile falls away, and she adds, "At least, with you, I'm not alone."

My heart squeezes, and I reach for her, pulling her flush to my chest in a fierce embrace. Maybe, if I can just hold her tight enough, the rest of the world won't be able to hurt her. Burying my face in her hair, I inhale the scent of her shampoo.

My cock stirs, already turned on by the way her body presses against mine.

I tilt her face up to mine and say fiercely, "Never. You will never be alone again."

My mouth crashes against hers, my urgency more like desperation to make my words true. Deep down, I know I can't promise that. Not when we're up against so much. But in this moment, all that exists is Lexi.

All that matters is showing her how I feel about her.

I kiss her like there's no tomorrow because there isn't. There's only today. This moment. Her body. Mine. The pleasure between us.

My hands trail her body, noting her curves and shape of her. She's fucking gorgeous, every inch of her, and while I want to see her without this dress on, I enjoy the way it clings to her now. My thumb brushes over her nipple, flicking it lightly, and she whimpers.

"Grey."

That single word is a plea for more, and it completely consumes me.

My cock hardens, painfully erect against my pants.

Without breaking our kiss, I grip her ass and lift her into the air. She gasps against my mouth then wraps her legs around my waist, her dress hiking up her thighs. With my palms cupping her ass, I carry her out of the kitchen and over to the couch, setting her gently on the center cushion.

On our left, the wall of glass offers a sparkling city

view—and the illusion that we're on full display for anyone to see.

"Are those windows—?"

"One-way glass," I assure her, though I can't deny I enjoy the idea that others might watch what I'm about to do to her. As long as they all know she's mine.

Lexi unwraps her legs from my waist, and I grip her thighs with my hands, parting them to reveal the slim strip of panties she's wearing underneath. She looks at me through lowered lashes, somehow both shy and daring me to keep going. It reminds me of the club when she gave me that lap dance. Maybe that's why I brought her here to the couch instead of taking her to my bedroom.

"What?" she asks, noting my expression.

"Feels a bit like role reversal," I say with a grin.

"Does that mean you're going to give me a lap dance?" she asks.

"I'm going to give you the same pleasure you gave me."

Her lips quirk, but I don't give her a chance to say anything else before I'm leaning in between her legs and pulling her panties aside to lick her pussy. Lexi gasps, her hand fisting in my hair as I stroke her clit with my tongue.

"Fuck, you taste amazing," I murmur.

Her scent, her taste, her presence—it's consuming in a way I've never felt before. I lose myself to the sensation of her on my tongue and the sounds she makes that tell me how she likes it. It doesn't take long before her thighs tense and tremble, and she arches her back, moaning as she comes against my mouth.

I don't stop, pushing her as high as she can go and

taking it all for myself. My wolf strains, urging me to bite her, claim her, but I grit my teeth, pulling back when the desire becomes too strong.

Instead, as she quiets again, I slide a finger inside her wet heat, stroking her lazily. She pants and leans forward, unclasping my belt. I let her do the work to unbutton my pants and free my throbbing cock.

She wraps her hand around my hard length, stroking me slowly, and I groan.

"I was wrong," I say. "You're the dangerous one."

She smirks as she uses her hand to guide my cock to her entrance. I push myself inside her then hiss at the way she contracts around me like a velvet vise.

"Fuck," I groan. "You feel so good."

I pull her hips to meet me, seating myself deep inside her, and she moans, her nails scraping my skin. Reaching up to grip the couch, I set a pace that has us both panting.

My wolf howls inside me, and the intensity of it combined with the ecstasy of our joined bodies sends me right to the edge.

Lexi makes a sound of pleasure, and her walls tighten around me.

I shove aside the urge to bite her, distracted by the sexy-as-fuck way she moves her body, rocking her hips to meet me. When her orgasm hits, she loses herself in it, and the thread of my control finally snaps.

My release slams into me, wave after wave. I tip my head back, shuddering as I ride it out. Lexi's hands on my chest bring me back. I look down at her, trying to catch my breath—overcome by the way it feels to be so fully owned by this woman. My cock buried inside her. Her name permanently etched on my heart.

I note the messy way her hair spills around her shoulders and the satisfied, relaxed expression she wears. My wolf feels proud of itself, the fucker.

"You felt all this pleasure that night at the club?" she asks, a teasing smile playing around her mouth.

"Pretty much. I had to finish up without you out back," I say, and she laughs. I cup her cheek with my hand and lean down to press a kiss to her mouth. "That club was sitting on a gold mine with you," I joke.

Her smile vanishes. "I was never for sale."

"No. You were never meant for anyone but me."

9

GREY

The last thing I want to do is get out of bed the next morning, especially with Lexi's ass pressed so deliciously against my erection, but I don't have a choice. Not unless I want to invite my father's wrath, and I'm well aware I need to choose my battles wisely. I kiss Lexi, whispering that she should sleep and spend the day relaxing. Then I reluctantly get up and get ready, reviewing the old man's orders.

Rather than any official pack business that might've presented an opportunity for gathering intel about his plans, he sends me on a day's worth of bullshit wedding errands: a tux fitting, an interview with some bachelor-themed blogger who wants to know what sort of porn I prefer, followed by a luncheon speech for the daughters of our city's fallen "militia"—code for mafia soldiers who died in the battle between our two feuding families.

Finally, he insists I have drinks with him and the generals at some sports bar where they get drunk and overly handsy with the waitstaff.

The only thing I learn is that Anthony Greco has a new position at the city treasurer's office. My father's over the moon about it.

"Everything's falling into place," he declares, raising his beer in a toast that the other generals echo.

Then they all drink and cheer like idiots.

By the time I manage to extricate myself, I'm exhausted and spiraling. A full day of my father's bullshit is bad enough, but then there are Lexi's secrets to figure out and Dutch's update earlier, which included a dead end on that plate he ran. At least, I receive confirmation that my package was delivered. Dutch sent me a picture of Dom's face as he opened the box. It's a grainy photo taken from a distance and through window blinds, but the disgust on the asshole's face is satisfying as fuck.

It's not nearly enough, but it'll have to do for now.

My phone rings right after I park in the garage, and I groan, dreading whatever bullshit thing my father wants me to do now. But the name on the caller ID is much more welcome.

"Hey, Mia," I say. "What's up?"

"Saw a clip of your speech earlier. Nice touch with the whole 'you're the city's real heroes' bit."

I smirk. "I might've laid it on a little thick."

"It's working. Between that and the social media accounts I'm running, the public is obsessed with you guys."

"Do I want to know about these accounts?"

"Relax. Dutch helped me set up some bots to re-post anything positive the media says about you guys. We're going with the hashtag Ley for your ship name. What do you think?"

"Subtle."

She laughs. "What did the old man say about your performance today?"

"He was already buzzed when I got to the bar after, but he thought it was good for PR."

"I bet he did. He still thinks all this is for him." She snickers. "What a fucking idiot. The public already loves you guys. It has nothing to do with him."

"Right now, I'm counting on him being slow on the uptake."

"Speaking of which, how's the alpha transformation coming?" she asks.

"Slow," I say with a sigh.

"Maybe we need to give it a push."

I don't bother telling her the one holding it back most is sitting upstairs in my penthouse. Lexi's secrets aren't just weighing her down—they're holding my wolf back. I'm not sure how much longer I can pretend she's not lying to me. Especially after last night.

"Maybe," I say. "Hey, did you hear back from Claire about the job reference?"

"Yeah," Mia says. "She's hired."

I exhale. "Good. Tell her we'll check in on her soon but to call if she needs anything else."

Claire's just the latest in a long line of girls Mia and I

helped get back on their feet after pulling them from the claws of the monsters this city calls leaders. Claire was Trucker's last victim, and the only thing I regret about killing him is doing it quickly. Hopefully, she can build a life for herself with this job at a local art gallery.

"Does your fiancée know you moonlight as a good Samaritan?"

"Nah. Ruins the image."

She chuckles. "Yeah, same here. Hey, has your dad mentioned anything about Lexi's medical history?"

"Why?"

"I had lunch with my dad today, hoping to get some intel, and I overheard him talking to Vincenzo about something to do with an illness Lexi had."

I frown. "He called last night and asked if she'd ever been sick."

"What did she say?"

"Once when she was a baby."

"What was the diagnosis?"

"She didn't say. I don't think she remembers."

She's silent for a beat before saying, "I think we should do the pack run."

I almost tell her no, that it's too dangerous. If we're discovered doing something like that without an official pack event, it'll give me away. But we're running out of time. My alpha needs a push. "Let's do it."

"Any idea where we can go that we won't be caught?"

"The ward line," I tell her. "Highway six. Give me a couple of hours."

"What about Lexi?"

"Maybe all of us shifting will trigger her wolf."

"Right." She snorts. "Like it's that easy."

I scowl. "Shut up."

"Bye, asshole."

"Later."

10

LEXI

I groan, dragged from sleep, thanks to an annoyingly incessant beeping. Groggy from great sex and the first good night of sleep I've had in ages, I look for the source of the noise. There—the phone on the nightstand. I crawl across Grey's side of the bed so I can reach it, surprised he hasn't walked into the room to grab it. Before I can do anything, it stops ringing.

I sigh, debating the merits of going back to sleep.

A note on the nightstand catches my eye. A scrawled message from Grey that he'll be back after he runs some errands.

Sleep it is.

I start to roll over as the phone rings again.

Frowning down at it, I debate what to do. I've used the damn thing so little that it takes several long moments for me to realize this is my phone, not Grey's.

The screen says the caller is unavailable.

Isn't Grey the only one with this number?

"Hello?" I answer uncertainly, my voice still heavy with sleep.

"It's about time." Ramsey's snarl sends my heart racing.

I sit up, looking around the room as if he can somehow see me. Suddenly, sleep is long gone. "How did you get this number?"

"Grey gave it to all of us," Ramsey says, sarcasm dripping from the words. "For your safety."

Right. Ramsey keeping me safe. What a joke.

"What do you want?" I demand.

"First, how about a thank you for saving your ass the other day at the pool house."

Fear is replaced by fury. "Saving my ass? Is that what you call it?"

"They would've eaten you alive if I hadn't twisted that story for us."

The casual way he's talking about that moment at Dutch's pool house has my hands curling into fists. "Keyword being *us*, asshole. If I go down, you go with me."

His tone sharpens. "Relax, no one's going down if you just do your job."

"I hate you," I snap.

"And I'm devastated about it. Now, what information do you have for me?"

I hesitate, my heart pounding. This is it. The moment of truth. I look down at the twist tie still twined around my ring finger, and my heart squeezes. I can't do this. I can't betray Grey. "I don't know anything you don't know."

"Bullshit. Grey spoke to Dutch about some kind of investigation he's doing. What are they looking into?"

"How do you know that?"

"Don't fucking worry about that. Answer the question. What's Dutch looking into?"

I frown, trying to decide whether to answer. But it's not anything that can hurt Grey. And I have to give him something. "We're trying to find out what happened to my wolf."

"What do you know so far?"

His question is so quick and urgent that I realize belatedly this is exactly the kind of information he wants after all. I think of what Serena said about my mom and the questions Vincenzo had about my medical history. No way I'm telling him any of that.

"Nothing."

"Don't fucking lie to me, Lexi. You know what happens if you don't come through on this."

"I'm not lying," I snap. "I still don't know anything. Believe me, if I did, I'd act on it. No one wants me to shift more than I do."

"What the hell are you waiting for then? If Grey won't do the job, I'm happy to fill in."

Unease ripples through me. "What job?"

"Come on," he says. "Don't tell me he hasn't told you."

"Told me what?" My anxiety spikes. "What the hell are you talking about?"

"A bite, Lexi. That's how you trigger a wolf that's been suppressed. He really hasn't mentioned it to you?"

My heart pounds as I consider his words. "You're

lying." Why would Grey keep something like that from me? Why wouldn't he just do it if it were that simple?

"Why would I do that?" he asks.

"Because you're jealous that Grey trusts me more than you. Because you're trying to control me by coming between me and him."

He scoffs. "You're controllable either way, believe me. Besides, you should be asking yourself why Grey hasn't mentioned it. Maybe he *doesn't* trust you after all. Maybe he's just biding his time until this wedding deal is done and then he'll get rid of you."

My cheeks heat. "I'm not talking about this with you."

"Fine. All that matters is what you can tell me about Grey's plans."

"Grey trusts you," I try again. "Your betrayal will hurt him so much. Don't you care about that? About him?"

"You just remember what will happen if you decide to mention our little arrangement," he says sharply.

He's quiet for a long moment, clearly waiting for me to give him the information he's asking for.

I bite my lip, refusing.

"You know," he says at last, "telling me would've been so much easier than the alternative." He sounds regretful, which is fake as hell but also puts me on edge.

"What's the alternative?"

"If you won't talk to me, you'll have to talk to Dom."

"No way," I say. "I have nothing to say to that asshole."

"You made a deal, Lexi. You gave your word that you'd find out what Grey's up to."

"You didn't give me any choice," I say.

"You think that fucking matters?" he snaps, his voice rising enough that I flinch. "If you don't have anything to say, I'm sure Dom will find another way to extract what's owed."

He ends the call, and my blood runs cold.

11

GREY

Just after five, I walk into the penthouse and find Lexi sprawled on the couch, watching a movie. My heart stutters at the sight of her in a pair of cotton shorts and a baggy shirt. Her hair is loose around her shoulders, and her face is clear of makeup.

She pauses the movie in the middle of some car chase and looks over at me as if I'm a riddle she can't solve. "Hey."

"Hey," I say casually, as if coming home to her isn't the most meaningful thing I've experienced in years.

What would it be like to go to some boring, normal-ass job all day and come home to this every night? What would I give to find out?

"How was your day?" she asks.

I pour myself a drink. "Fucked up. How was yours?"

She watches warily as I cross to the couch. When she

starts to move her feet out of the way, I grab her ankles with my free hand, lifting them so I can sit. Then I place her feet in my lap, massaging them as I sip my drink.

She relaxes slightly, still studying me. "Thoughtful," she finally answers.

I look over at her, something about her tone putting me on alert. "Did something happen?"

"You mean aside from last night?" She smiles ruefully, and I note that she's sitting in the exact spot I had her in.

My cock twitches at the reminder. I run my hand farther up her leg. "Is that what you thought about all day?"

"Well, some," she admits, her cheeks going slightly pink. It's arousing as fuck.

"And the rest?"

Her expression shifts to something more serious. "I don't think we're doing enough to trigger my wolf."

I frown. Whatever I was expecting, it's not this. "What makes you say that?"

"I know you're looking into it, but so far, we've uncovered nothing."

"It's only been a few days," I point out, but my thoughts drift to my father's questions about Lexi's medical history.

He knows something we don't. I just wish I knew what. So far, Dutch's hacking has yielded nothing.

"Grey, this wedding's coming fast. We have no idea what your dad's planning to do after we take those vows. For all I know, he's going to kill me. And I need to be able to defend myself. Especially if I'm going to stay here. With you."

"You won't need to defend yourself. I'm not going to let anyone get close enough that you would even need to fight."

"You can't promise something like that."

I bite back my frustration. She's right. I can't promise that. If I could, my father wouldn't already have his hooks in us this deeply. Besides, she deserves her wolf. I can't even imagine not having access to mine.

Plus, explaining how mates work would be a hell of a lot easier if she could feel the bond too. But the only way I know to trigger her wolf is through a bite. And if it doesn't work... I can't take that chance.

"Did Dutch find out anything about the license plate?" she presses.

I sigh. "No. It was a dead end."

"Dammit." She sits back, clearly frustrated.

I frown, hating that she's so upset. "But—it just so happens, I already planned to take you out tonight and work on triggering your wolf."

"Really?" She pulls her feet off my lap and sits up straighter. "What's the plan? What are we waiting for?"

"Whoa, chill. We're going to meet the others and do a pack run."

"How can I run if I'm not a wolf yet?"

"Well, I'm hoping seeing the others in wolf form might help trigger yours."

Her excitement turns to wariness. "Is that safe for me? Being around them all in their wolf forms?"

"Of course. None of the others would ever hurt you."

She looks away.

I frown. What the hell am I missing here? "If you don't want to go…"

"No, I do," she says quickly. When I don't respond, she pushes to her feet, standing in front of me with her hands on her hips. I note her very short shorts and tank top.

"Bring a jacket," I tell her. "And leave your phone."

"Done."

She hurries down the hall to the bedroom. A moment later, she returns wearing a hoodie that threatens to swallow her whole. Her legs are bare, and the hoodie is large enough that it looks like she's not wearing pants. I drink in the sight of her bare skin, imagining running my hands over her body.

Oblivious, she walks to the elevator and slides her feet into a pair of sandals I bought for her. "Ready," she announces.

Her enthusiasm has an edge to it, but I don't say anything as we ride the elevator down to the garage. We both get into the car, and I stop long enough to snap an order at my guards. "Don't follow us."

They start to protest, but I gun it, squealing tires drowning them out as we peel off into the night.

"Will they tell your dad?" Lexi asks, looking perfectly calm about the fact that I'm driving like a lunatic.

"I don't know."

"What if they catch up to us?"

I press the gas a little harder, accelerating around a tight corner. "They won't."

I drive through the city way too fast, running two red

lights before I manage to get us out of downtown. When I'm convinced we're not being followed, I speed down the empty road that leads out of town. I begin to calm once the buildings fall away and the suburbs disappear. By the time we hit the open highway, the streetlights are all behind us, and the darkness presses in.

My skin itches from the inside. Now that I've made the decision to run, my wolf is impatient to be free.

"Where are we going?" she asks.

"To the walls of this cage," I tell her.

It doesn't take long before the familiar sign comes into view. To anyone else, it's a normal mile marker. But those from Indigo Hills know better. I pull over just behind it, slamming on the brakes hard enough to kick up gravel in our wake.

Out here, we're finally truly alone.

"Where are the others?" Lexi asks.

"They'll be here soon. We're early. Come on." I climb out of the car.

Escaping the city has calmed me, but it doesn't appease the urge to let the beast inside me take over. He wants to feel the fresh air on his fur. To see his mate through his own eyes.

Soon.

Lexi climbs out of the car and rounds the hood, stopping before me. She looks so fucking small inside that hoodie—which I now realize is mine.

"That's my hoodie," I say.

"Yeah." She looks almost sheepish.

"Why are you wearing it when I just bought you all those clothes?"

"Because it smells like you."

I stare at her, relishing the answer. "You like the way I smell?"

"Yeah." She dips her head but not before I see her cheeks go pink. Her reaction is both sweet and sexy, and I'm getting hard just watching her.

Refusing to let myself get sucked in, I turn to the mile marker. "Do you know what that is?"

"A road sign marking the highway miles?"

"Walk over to it."

"Why?"

"I want to show you something." I wait until she gets to the sign then looks back at me. "Touch it."

She bites her lip but does as I say. The moment her fingertips touch the sign, it zaps her, and she jumps back, holding her fingers to her lips.

She stares at me accusingly. "What the hell?"

"Indigo Hills is surrounded by powerful wards put here centuries ago by witches. Hexerei, they called themselves. We're taught the wards are for our protection—to keep the rest of the world out of our business and to keep them from trying to hurt us. But the truth is, the wards are just as good at keeping us in as they are at keeping the world out."

"This is what's trapping me here," she says.

"We're all trapped here."

Her brows scrunch. "How did you leave to get me then?" she asks. "And how did I get into the city in the first place?"

"The wards can be programmed to allow people in and out. But only an alpha can come and go freely, and only an alpha can alter them."

"Your father let you out," she says. "And let me in."

I nod.

She tilts her head. "What about five years ago?" she asks. "When you left town?"

"My father let me go," I say quietly.

"Really? He seems so angry about you being gone."

I hesitate as painful memories come rushing back. "It's a long story."

A pair of headlights wink into view along the highway.

"Maybe later," Lexi says as Dutch pulls up behind us with Razor and Crow in the backseat.

Behind them, Mia and Ramsey arrive.

The sound of their voices fills the night as they all climb out and greet one another.

"Who's ready for a night run?" Dutch calls out.

Razor howls. "I bet you fifty bucks I'm faster than you tonight," he calls out to Crow.

"You're fucking on, slowpoke," Crow shoots back.

Even Mia laughs and adds her bet to Crow's side of things. Their excitement sings in my veins. In my wolf's blood.

Lexi watches it all with wary anticipation.

"Hey, Lex," Mia calls out. "You feeling wolfy yet?"

Dutch snorts. "Is that the technical term?"

Mia flips him off. "As a matter of fact, yes."

Lexi shakes her head.

"You okay with this?" I ask her quietly.

"Yeah."

"You sure?"

She rolls her eyes. "I'm not going to faint again."

I grin and kiss her cheek. "Please don't. They'll never let you live it down."

12

LEXI

I stand beside Grey's car, trying not to be obvious as he strips out of his clothes, but it's hard to look away. First, because his naked body is mouth-wateringly hot. But once the change starts, my fascination is for entirely different reasons.

His back arches then curves as bones pop and crack. He grimaces, but in the next moment, his flesh becomes fur, and he's no longer a man.

An enormous gray wolf stares back at me soundlessly. I watch him warily. He won't hurt me, but knowing it and seeing a giant predator standing before me are two different things.

Movement catches my eye, and I look over as five more wolves appear from around the cars. Mia's wolf is the most recognizable with its coppery fur and long, lean build. She gives me a familiar look then trots up beside Grey and huffs impatiently.

Behind her trails a golden-yellow wolf with large, bright eyes that glare at me. Ramsey.

I do my best to ignore him entirely and focus on the others.

There's a large chestnut wolf whose saunter clearly belongs to Dutch. Behind him, Razor and Crow are indistinguishable, their matching mahogany coats and thick bodies making them twins in this form. Instead of joining the rest of them, Razor nips at Crow's haunches, who immediately tackles him in retaliation, and they go rolling in the dirt.

Mia snarls at them both, and I can't help but smile.

It's kind of wild how easily their personalities shine through even as wolves.

When I look back at Grey, he's watching me steadily. I hold his gaze, fighting the overwhelm at being the object of such intense focus from a deadly predator. But unlike the first time he shifted in front of me, I'm not overcome with fear.

If anything, I feel utterly protected under his scrutiny.

His eyes glow in the darkness, and he watches me patiently. Probably waiting to make sure I'm not going to freak out on him.

"Go," I urge him. "I'm fine."

He huffs then tilts his head back and howls. A moment later, the others echo the sound. Even Razor and Crow stop wrestling to join in.

The sound is mournful and seeps all the way into my bones, stirring me with a strange sort of yearning. Like my body wants something from me, though I have no idea how to give it. My breath catches. Is this it?

Is this the moment my wolf will finally come out?

Nothing happens.

The song finally ends, and the six wolves take off into the valley at a dead run. Grey leads, his massive paws eating up the ground at an impossible pace. Dutch falls in behind Grey, and the others fan out around him.

I watch until long after they're out of sight. When they're gone, I stare up at the sky, noting the way the stars wink brightly across the canopy stretched above me. It's beautiful in a way I've never experienced living in the city. Even Lakeland, a small town compared to Indigo Hills, didn't offer me a moment like this. Then again, maybe it's more about having found somewhere to belong than the sky itself.

A few minutes later, a single wolf reappears in the distance. Grey. He's alone, leaving me to wonder if he's that much faster than the others or if they're content to run without him. His speed makes him nothing more than a blur until he comes to a stop not far from me, panting and watching me just as intently as before.

He takes a step forward.

My skin buzzes with a strange sensation.

He takes another step, and the buzzing gets stronger.

Excitement and anticipation rise inside me. I brace myself for the same transformation I saw in Grey's body when he became a wolf.

But again, nothing happens.

Finally, I put my hand out. His wolf closes the distance, rubbing against my bare leg. Tentatively, I run a hand along his fur. It's softer than I expected. I scratch his ear, which earns me a strange growling sound that makes me smile.

The others finally return with Mia in the lead. Razor is on her heels with Dutch and Crow shoulder to shoulder behind them. They race toward Grey before coming to a stop just behind him, standing much closer to me than they were before.

My blood pumps faster, adrenaline suddenly coursing through me. I glance from Grey to the others, my body tensing. My breath comes in shorter bursts, and my hands fist at my sides as I study the distance between Grey and the others.

Too close.

My throat constricts as I fight the urge to scream at them to get away.

I don't even realize my reaction is noticeable until the wolf whose fur I'd been clutching a moment ago is suddenly gone and Grey's wrapping human arms around me. "It's okay," he says, his voice soothing.

I push him away, but that only makes it worse as my hands press against his bared skin. My head swims with dizziness and confusion. "I don't feel good."

Heat works its way up from my legs to my torso, flushing my face. I'm aware they're all watching me as if they're waiting for something. Maybe it's my wolf.

The thought is both welcome and terrifying.

"Just breathe," Grey says.

But I can't. My jaw clenches until I'm gritting my teeth against the urge to attack Mia for standing way too close to Grey.

I don't think this is my wolf.

"I think… I need them to leave."

Grey's brow lifts, but he nods. "Done." He turns to the others. "We'll talk tomorrow."

All five of them head for their cars.

A moment later, I can hear the rumble of voices as they shift back and dress. Then, one by one, they get into their cars and drive away.

When they're gone, I concentrate on trying to breathe, but my thoughts are consumed by the realization that Grey and I are alone out here—and he's gloriously naked.

Before I can overthink it, I peel the hoodie off, revealing my tiny tank top underneath.

"What are you doing?" Grey asks, but he doesn't look confused.

If anything, his expression is hungry.

Exactly how I feel.

I peel my tank off and let it drop next to my shorts. "I need you," I tell him. "Now."

When he doesn't move fast enough, I close the distance, kissing him with a ferocity that shocks me. But I don't stop. He puts his arms around me, tangling his hands in my hair for a moment before roaming my body: caressing my back in a slow, smooth sweep, squeezing my hips, brushing his thumbs over my ribs, cupping handfuls of my breasts. I wrap my arms around his neck, pressing myself against him with a need that has me whimpering for more.

He responds with a growl and picks me up, carrying me over and setting me on the hood of the car. It's warm on my skin, but I scoot to the edge, wanting only the heat that Grey can provide. He crowds between my open legs, eliminating any space between our bodies as his mouth claims mine. His tongue parts my lips, sweeping into my mouth and invading my senses.

Heat pools at my core, an ache that pulses inside me—a need I can't think past.

He finds my breast again, his thumb flicking my hardened nipple. Then his hand trails lower, dipping inside my panties until he's running his fingers between my wet folds.

The sensations ignite me, and I arch my hips to meet his strokes, moaning against his mouth.

"More," I demand.

He kisses a trail down my jawline and throat, burying his face in my neck and inhaling deeply as he slides a finger inside me.

Desire lashes through me, and I shudder at the intensity of it.

Grey adds another finger, pushing them into me with a delicious pressure, and I moan as his mouth finds mine again. With my arms around his neck, I rock against him, meeting his rhythm.

It's not enough.

I need all of him.

"Please," I whisper, ready to beg if that's what it takes.

"What do you want, Lexi?" he asks in a low voice.

He slows the rhythm of his fingers, which only makes me ache for more.

"Tell me what you want," he says.

"I want you," I say, breathless and so fucking desperate for him.

Before he can answer, I reach for his cock. It's hard and thick as I wrap my hand around it, stroking it.

He hisses out a breath against my lips, and pleasure rockets through me knowing I'm the one teasing him now.

"This is what I want," I say, bold in a way I've never been before.

"Fuck," he groans, sliding his fingers out of me and lifting me to my feet so quickly I make a noise of surprise. "Hold on," he orders.

He yanks my panties down and nearly rips them trying to get them off my ankles. Then he's setting me back on the warm hood of the car and pressing the tip of his erection against my entrance.

"This?" he asks, his voice thick with a need that thrums in my own veins.

"Yes," I pant. "Please."

With a growl, he sheaths himself inside me, and I gasp at the sudden explosion of sensation. Slowly, he slides nearly out again, and I feel myself contract around him.

All at once, he slams into me again, and the pace is set. I grip his shoulders, holding on and meeting his strokes as my pleasure builds. The fact that we're sitting out in the open, where anyone could drive up and see us, only adds to the thrill.

Grey's gaze grows darker and darker as he thrusts into me. I can see the tension building inside him, and it only makes me want to drive him higher. The furious jealousy from earlier is gone. In its place, I feel a tug in my chest—like some sort of cord has been loosed, connecting us. There's no time to understand it as my pleasure sends me careening toward the edge.

Grey's eyes are intent and knowing, and I can't help but feel that he senses this cord binding us too—and welcomes it.

"That's it, darling. Give me everything you have," he coaxes.

The cord in my heart yanks harder, and I fly up and over the edge as I come for him.

His name is a broken cry on my lips as my orgasm sends me soaring.

Grey's body tenses. He grips my hair, pulling my face to his until we're eye to eye, so close I can feel his breath. "Mine," he growls; then his body shudders, and he comes hard.

I cling to him, riding out the aftershocks until we're both quiet.

Grey kisses me softly, leaning his forehead against mine. With my eyes closed, I breathe him in, enjoying the way it feels to be in his arms like this. My heart rate finally slows, and I take a deep, steadying breath before pulling back to look at him.

His smile is soft and genuine.

The earlier hunger is gone; sated…for now.

But I can't help trying to make sense of the strange tug I felt earlier. It could've just been a sex thing, except that I still feel it even now. Faint, but there. I'm afraid he'll think I'm crazy, so I don't say anything. But in my heart, I know that whatever connection we just made, it's unbreakable.

13

GREY

Lexi's arms are draped over my shoulders, her forehead resting against mine. This moment feels like the closest thing to peace I've had in weeks. It's not just the orgasm or the fact that my wolf had some freedom tonight. It's knowing Lexi felt the mate bond. Her scent was full of untamed jealousy earlier. A possessiveness that could only come from the mate call.

Her wolf is in there, I'm sure of it. And as soon as it's freed, I'm going to claim her as mine.

I pull my forehead away from hers and study her in the darkness. "How are you feeling?"

Her cheeks flush. "Better. I don't know what came over me."

I could tell her, but I don't. Not yet. Not until I can bite her without possibly killing her.

"Your wolf," I say distractedly, leaning in to inhale the

smell of her throat—which is really just another form of torture at this point.

"What about it?" she asks, breathless all over again.

I straighten, an idea forming. "Can I try something?"

"What?" she asks warily.

"Do you remember when my father suppressed my wolf?"

She winces. "At the lake house. Yes. It looked painful."

"It was. But it makes me wonder… Maybe that's what happened to you?"

"You think someone suppressed my wolf? How would that work?"

"Someone—an alpha—would've commanded your wolf to recede into the background. With an order."

"Wouldn't I feel it though? You seemed pretty upset over not being able to access your wolf. Like you were still aware of it inside you."

"Yes," I admit. "It's why I haven't tried it before now. But there are signs that your wolf is in there."

"Is that what I felt tonight?" she asks.

"Yes." It's not the whole truth, but it's a start.

She bites her lip. "How can the order be undone?"

"Only by another alpha." Or a mate. "Can I try it?"

She swallows hard. "Okay."

I brace myself, hoping like hell this works. After tonight, my alpha power is stronger than it's ever been. If this is what happened to her wolf, I'm strong enough to undo it now.

"Liberum lupus."

A moment passes.

Then two.

Nothing.

I sigh.

Lexi smiles, but it's strained. "It's okay. That would've felt way too easy, honestly."

I shake my head, frustrated. "We're running out of time. My father's digging for answers, too, and if he gets them first, it could be dangerous."

"You think there's more to his plan than just forcing us to get married?"

"I think the marriage was just another way to take something from me," I say quietly. "It was more about cruelty than strategy."

"What do you mean?"

"If we're married, as your husband, even if you relinquish your title, I'd be next in line for alpha. That means he has to take your title from us both."

She shakes her head, the disgust in her expression plain. "Why? I mean, I know he's an asshole, but you make it sound like he has a vendetta against you."

I hesitate but only to find the right words to tell her this story—one she should know before things get any crazier. "Five years ago, Franco came to me. He knew how I felt about my old man, and he offered a solution. He asked me to spy on my father. To feed him information about Vincenzo's plans for a takeover."

She stares at me like she's seen a ghost, so I look away from her and concentrate on the words. On getting them out without getting sucked into the agony of reliving that time—and everything it cost me—all over again.

"By then, I'd come to know my father for the monster he truly is. It wasn't just the way he ran his pack or his businesses. I'd seen that and somehow found a way to look past it. But my mother…he hurt her. Many times. I'd always suspected, but when I finally saw it for myself…"

Finishing that sentence would mean letting those images play out in my memory, and I can't. So, I push past them to what came next.

"If my wolf had been stronger, I could've challenged him outright. But I knew I couldn't win a fight against an alpha. Franco offered another way. But it backfired."

"How?" She's riveted on me now. Hanging on every word.

I wish the story ended better for her sake. For all of ours.

"Franco ordered me to lace my father's drink with some chemical. Said it would weaken him enough for whatever he had planned. Said I would know when to do it. Two nights later, Dom's older brother Tio challenged my father for the role of alpha of our pack. My father was smug as hell about it. His ego blinded him to the idea that he might lose, but I knew this was the moment Franco had meant.

"The day of the fight, I made my father a drink with the drug in it. He never suspected me. Drank it all without hesitation. By that night, he was too weak to do more than stand. I braced myself for his death. Prepared for it as much as one can, I guess. Told myself the city would be better, safer. My mom would be safer."

"Then what happened?"

"Right before the fight began, my father announced that he was nominating a champion to fight in his place." The bleakness closes in around me as I remember it all over again. The shock. The horrible realization that I would have to face Tio for him. That he would survive this, and I might not.

"Was that allowed?" Lexi asks.

"According to some old, forgotten pack law. No one remembered it existed until my father cited it. Almost as if he knew ahead of time."

"Who did he name as his champion?"

"Me."

"Oh." Her eyes widen as she realizes where this is going. How it all must've ended. "You fought Tio?"

"Yes."

"And you won."

"Yes."

"Did he…? Did you…?"

"I killed him. It's the code. An alpha challenge is a fight to the death."

"But…if you won, you should be alpha."

"I fought on behalf of my father. My victory belonged to him, ensuring he remains in his role." I can't help the self-loathing that leaks into my voice. "What a fucking double agent I made, huh? I sabotaged my own efforts. It was all a fucking waste."

She stares at me.

I can see the wheels turning, but I'll be damned if I can tell in which direction they're going. Maybe she hates me now. Maybe seeing me as a killer—or worse, a traitor—

has changed her view of me. Have I finally scared her off with the fucked-up reality of what it's like to be me?

"That's why he called you back here?" Her voice is full of outrage. "Why he's making you marry me then taking everything from us both? It's all about his sick revenge."

Her disgust is for him—my father.

Not for me.

Relief washes over me.

"He considers it justice," I say.

"He's a fucking monster."

She's angry, and I love her for it.

"We have to find out what happened to your wolf before he does," I tell her.

She looks up at me, her expression reflecting the determination I feel. "We're going to find a way. And then we're going to stop him and Franco from ever hurting anyone again."

She's naively hopeful, and I don't have the heart to tell her it's a long shot. The way she's looking at me now… No one's ever looked at me like that before. But it only matters that Lexi does.

"Hopefully, you're right, but if we fail, we'll come here," I tell her, framing her face with my hands. "To these wards. So we can get the hell out of this city."

"I thought you couldn't get out unless an alpha allows it?"

"Yes, well, that's the difference between this fight and the one five years ago. I'm an alpha now. Soon, I'll be strong enough to save us both."

14

GREY

I don't want to bring Lexi with me today, but my father texted me early this morning and ordered it. The fact that he wants me to do something so risky suggests he's feeling confident about his position. This morning's paper featured another article and more photos from our date the other night, including the interview quotes from each of us as we entered the restaurant. Clearly, he's pleased about us winning points with the public. But he's a fool if he thinks that gives him carte blanche to walk an outsider into a meeting like this one.

Then again, he's not walking her in. I am. And she's not an outsider. She's Franco's granddaughter, which, technically speaking, means she has a right to attend.

Or that's what I tell myself as I shower and put on a suit. In the mirror, I check for any imperfections—if I don't fix them now, they'll be used against me later. Inspecting myself carefully, I straighten my tie with a quick tug. And even though I don't spot a single wrinkle, I smooth the fabric out of habit anyway. I make myself a promise: When I take over this city, I'll never wear a suit again.

It's a small comfort.

There's nothing to be done about the darkness that lingers in my eyes or the circles beneath them.

Fuck it.

Even monsters can look tired, I guess.

My phone buzzes with a text.

Crow's message is quick and to the point, as usual. *Nothing to report from Greece.*

He's texted me the same update ever since I had him start following Ramsey. Maybe there's nothing there.

Maybe I'm just being paranoid.

If he was bound to me, I'd know for sure.

I think of the blade stashed inside a hard case in the warehouse but dismiss the thought as quickly as it comes. Using it would mean giving myself away as an alpha. Am I ready for what I'd have to do next?

When I emerge, Lexi's standing in the kitchen in nothing but my t-shirt, holding a mug of coffee. She looks rumpled from sleep and so damn fuckable. I walk right over to her and weave my hands into her hair so I can tilt her head back and kiss her deeply.

She melts against me, offering up whatever I want to take from her. Which is everything. Starting with bending her over the counter right here and now.

She'd let me. I can feel it in her already hardened nipples and the way she's rubbing herself against me. And maybe I should. Burying myself inside her would probably go a long way toward helping me prepare mentally for today. But we can't afford to be late. Not for this.

I reluctantly let her go, adjusting myself.

"Good morning," she says, smiling up at me with swollen lips.

"Morning," I say in a voice that's probably not as warm as she deserves, but it's the best I can do right now. My stress is always higher on meeting days, but bringing Lexi into the mix has me tenser than usual.

"You look nice," she says as her gaze slides over my suit questioningly, and my balls tighten at the compliment. I shake off my fantasies of stripping us both down to nothing and force myself to refocus.

"I'm headed out for a meeting."

"Oh." Her expression falls, which makes bringing her even easier—and more torturous.

"Would you like to come with me?"

She brightens. "Do I need to dress up?"

"It would be best. The generals will be there. And my father. It's an official mafia pack meeting, and my father requested you join us."

"I see." Now, her excitement is tempered. That's smart. She sets her mug aside, her chin lifting with a bravery I'm sure she doesn't even recognize in herself. "I'll go get ready."

I don't move as she walks past me. Her scent washes over me, but my control is absolute. It's not until her bedroom door shuts that I make a beeline for the living room where I put on music to drown out the sound of her running the shower. Anything to keep from picturing her naked on the other side of that wall.

Since our trip out to the ward line last night, the mate call has grown stronger. My desire for her—along with my hunger to bite and claim her—is almost unbearable now. The only thing holding me back is her safety. If I bite her and she doesn't survive it… I couldn't live with that.

My phone rings. When I see who it is, I answer quickly. "What's up?"

"We need to chat about what happened last night," Mia says.

"Which part?"

"The part where she basically went into heat right in front of us."

"I'm not talking about this right now."

"You and I both know there's a way to trigger her wolf."

"It's not guaranteed."

"You're right. It only works if her wolf is strong, and considering she almost attacked an entire wolf pack to defend her claim on your dick, I'd say it is."

"You don't know for sure," I snap.

There's a beat of silence before she says, "Is that why you haven't claimed her yet? You're scared of the bite?"

"I don't want to talk about this right now," I say, my voice a warning.

"She's a human in a shifter war. We can't afford that kind of liability."

"She's a liability as a wolf," I say.

"What are you—"

"The moment she's a wolf, my father won't hesitate to compel her with alpha power. He'll control her completely."

"Unless you're her alpha," she points out.

"I'm not ready yet." I swallow hard then take a deep breath. "This is how I keep her safe."

Mia sighs. "She's a target either way, Grey."

"All my father wants is her title."

"Bullshit. He wants more—he always wants more."

She's right, of course. But I don't admit that. If I do, I'll have to admit she's right about everything else. That the only way to save Lexi is to do something that might kill her. "I need to get going, or I'll be late."

"This conversation isn't over."

I end the call, silently arguing with myself about Mia's warning. Lexi would be stronger as a wolf—and more vulnerable. The indecision is twisting me up inside.

Half an hour later, Lexi rejoins me. "Does this look okay?"

She's wearing a navy blue sheath dress. It's simple, elegant, and sensible. There's absolutely no reason I should be rock-hard at the sight of her in it. And yet, I adjust myself discreetly behind the kitchen counter before setting my coffee mug in the sink and rounding to where she waits.

"It's perfect," I tell her, my voice embarrassingly hoarse.

She moves to walk by me, but I reach for her, pulling her against my chest. This close, I smell her freshly soaped skin and, beneath that, the scent that makes her unique—and irresistible.

Her lips part invitingly, her pulse speeding. "We could skip it," she says as my mouth brushes hers.

I groan.

It takes everything in me to pull away from her.

"When we get home," I tell her, gripping her hips possessively, "I'm going to take that dress off you with my teeth."

She shivers, her smirk more like a dare. "I look forward to it."

Fuck.

"Come on," I say, propelling us to the elevator before I can change my mind.

"So, what's the meeting about?" she asks as we ride the elevator downstairs. I bypass the garage and instead take us to the lobby's main exit where Elio, one of the men assigned to my security detail, has our car waiting.

It's best to keep up the expected pretenses, which include allowing myself to be driven to these things.

"Grey?" Lexi asks as we cross the lobby.

"Hmm?"

"Is everything okay?"

"These meetings aren't my favorite," I say, and she nods like she gets it.

She doesn't.

Outside, the morning sun is bright and hot, promising to bake the city before the day is done. Lexi looks up at it, angling her face as if to soak it in before she ducks into the car ahead of me. With a nod at Elio, I slide into the cool interior behind her.

I don't bother to check behind us for Cruz and Darius since I already know they'll follow us over.

"What do I need to know about this meeting?" Lexi asks.

"It's a full pack meeting," I start.

"Okay. I've met them all before," she says, "and your dad's currently happy with us, so that's a good start. What else?"

"The meeting includes the entire Indigo Hills mafia pack leadership," I explain. "It won't just be my father and our generals."

"Franco will be there," she says, eyes widening as understanding dawns.

"And his generals," I add.

Her bravado slips, and her cheeks pale. "Dom."

I nod. "And a couple others you haven't met yet."

"Do I have to be there?" she asks nervously.

"My father wants you there, but technically, the answer is no," I tell her. "In fact, there might be a few complaints that I've brought you, considering we're not married yet and you haven't been officially recognized as Franco's heir." My gaze flicks to the ring she's wearing.

She twists it nervously, though I don't think she realizes she's doing it. "Then why did you?"

"Well, my father suggested it."

"But?" she prompts.

"But the truth is that I brought you because I can protect you better if you're with me."

She doesn't protest my reasoning. Nor does she point out how caged that must make her feel. I don't add that she deserves to see how things work in my world, to see what she's gotten herself into. Or that I'm double checking that she meant what she said about wanting to stay in this city with me.

Maybe that's why I haven't told her about the mate thing yet. Maybe I'm waiting to see if she changes her mind about the life I'm asking her to live with me.

Fuck, maybe I'm the one with trust issues here.

"Will Dutch and the others be there?" she asks.

"Mia and Ramsey will. Their dads have begun training them for their future positions."

Her brow creases. "The others aren't being trained?"

"Rocco wants to train Dutch, but my father refuses."

"Why?"

I sigh. "He suspects Dutch knew about my failed coup five years ago. He doesn't fully trust him."

"Did he?"

My thoughts darken at the memory of that time. "He covered my trail so my father wouldn't know where I went or how to find me."

"And Razor and Crow?"

My mouth lifts. Telling her this one cheers me up. "Alvaro invited Razor, but he refused to come unless Crow's invited too."

She matches my half-smile. "Good."

"Listen," I say, sobering quickly, "what you'll see in there... It's not going to be pretty."

"I don't expect it to be."

"The thing is they're monsters who get off on hurting people, but they're also just enforcing what we consider our laws. So, it's not something we can talk them out of."

"Okay."

"What I mean is—"

"Grey." She lays her hand over mine. "I'm walking into a room full of the most ruthless predators to walk the earth. I'm not expecting an ice cream social."

Her smile's probably meant to put me at ease, but it only makes me more certain I should've left her at home.

Too late.

The car pulls to a stop in front of GV Industries, the high-rise that houses Franco's professional offices and serves as the pack's headquarters. The sound of raised voices draws my attention, and I glance out the tinted windows to the street beyond. The sidewalk in front of the building is already lined with reporters blocking the doors so they can get a clear shot of us before we go inside. I was expecting that. What I didn't expect was the crowd assembled across the street, many holding posters and signs and chanting words too muffled to make out.

One of the signs reads *Expose the Scandal*. Another says *Stop Stealing From Our Kids*.

"What's going on over there?" Lexi asks.

"Looks like a protest," I say, frowning. "Word must've gotten out that school funds are missing."

"Missing?"

"Re-allocated," I say, shaking my head as my temper spikes hot. "Franco probably decided he needed another mountain cabin."

Recently, Dutch dug up proof of a huge chunk of tax money being siphoned into the Giovanni Foundation—Franco's supposed charity, which mostly operates as a smokescreen for laundering more than his share of city funds back to himself. According to Dutch's hacking, some of that money was meant for the local schools' music and arts programs.

Apparently, Dutch and I aren't the only ones who've put the pieces together. Citizens of Indigo Hills aren't stupid; it was only a matter of time until they figured it out. But protesting in the street—in front of Franco's building, at that—isn't going to win their cause any points.

Before I can explain it all to Lexi, Elio opens my door.

I hesitate as the protestors' chanting hits me.

"Fund our schools! Fund our schools!"

Lexi nudges me, and I shove my worry for these people aside as I climb out. Cameras and reporters are waiting for us, but for once, they're not here for quotes about the happy couple's pending nuptials. This is pack business, plain and simple, and they all want to broadcast or headline the main events. The public thrives on news, even when it's sadistic. Especially then.

Lexi joins me on the sidewalk just as another limo pulls to a stop behind ours. Mia and Charlie Reyes get out. Lexi hesitates, waiting for Mia, but I grab her hand and pull her along.

"Not now," I say quietly.

Mia doesn't even look over at us as she tosses her hair for the paparazzi. Beside her, Charlie Reyes looks past everyone like he's above it all. Including Lexi and me.

I let him stride by us before leading Lexi toward the doors.

Behind us, Mia pauses to give an interview. I don't hear what she says, but the reporters all roar with laughter.

Inside, the air is cool, the sounds from the street muted. Everything about GV Industries is clean and white and perfectly polished. I'm not surprised or fooled by it. The blood of Franco's sins isn't here; it's on his hands.

Lexi sticks close as we enter the building's auditorium just off the main atrium. Inside, several others have already arrived.

I nod at Ramsey seated beside his father. He gives a quick raise of his chin, his gaze sliding from me to Lexi. His brow quirks at the sight of her. It's the only indication of surprise or concern he offers.

We won't speak here.

Not in front of so many witnesses.

With Lexi's hand in mine, I climb the steps toward the higher rows, choosing a seat where I can look down on the crowd rather than have an enemy at my back. Lexi settles in next to me, and my leg warms where hers presses against it. It's a comforting feeling, having her touching me, but I don't let myself look at her. Instead, I scan the rows of seating below, taking inventory of the players.

My father is seated up front, as usual, his back to me. He and Alvaro have their heads bent in some private conversation. Suddenly, my father stops talking and looks up—directly at me. His eyes narrow when he spots Lexi beside me. His mouth hardens. It's an angry look I don't understand, considering he's the one who suggested she come today, but he finally turns back to Alvaro and resumes his conversation, effectively shutting me out.

I exhale and tear my eyes from the asshole to look at the others nearby.

My mother sits in the third row beside the other generals' wives. Even from here, she looks stiff and closed off. She hates these things almost more than she hates being married to my father.

Franco made attendance mandatory for alpha's mates and their offspring right around the time I began spying for him. He can't take it back now without looking weak, which leaves me with enough gray area to have Lexi here today. If he balks at it, he'll only look like a fool.

Or that's my theory.

It could go the other way, and he rejects her as his heir and names Dom instead. But I'm banking on the element of surprise working in my favor.

Slow and quiet.

Chipping away at them from all angles until their authority is gone.

That's how we'll fight.

Even as I think it, the alpha in me stirs.

"Are those Franco's generals?" Lexi asks, pointing.

I nod, looking at the trio of men all seated in the second row on the right. "That's Santiago on the left with the gray hair," I say. "And beside him is his brother Conrad. They've been with Franco since they were kids. The one with the tattoos is Toros. He used to be the leader of a street gang here in Indigo Hills called The Bane, who fought against the corruption of the alpha regime."

"Seriously? How did he end up as Franco's general?" she asks.

"When the gang became powerful enough to be a threat to Franco's status quo, he made Toros an offer to join him or be destroyed."

I don't tell her what a fucking disappointment it was to learn Toros had turned. Or how close Dutch and I came to reaching out to The Bane to form an alliance right before Toros switched sides. That would've been a fucking mess.

It's also the reason I can't count on anyone else to help us do this. We have to do it alone—which means we have to do it right. As a bonded pack.

"Who are the women seated in the row behind them? And the ones next to your mother?"

"Gloria is next to my mom," I explain. "She's Alvaro's wife."

Gloria turns to glance behind her at the back of the room. Lexi studies her, saying, "Razor's mom? Wow, he looks just like her."

"Don't tell him that," I warn her. "They're not close. And beside her is Sonesta. She's married to Rocco."

I don't know either of them very well as they've managed to remain firmly in the background of their husbands' lives over the years. Probably more for survival than anything else. But they always attend these meetings and keep to themselves when they do.

Smart.

"So, Sonesta is Dutch's mom?" she asks.

I nod. "You look surprised."

"I guess I just didn't realize those assholes had managed to find a woman to stick with them."

My lips twitch because, in a room full of shifters, I can guarantee her words are carrying. But I still explain, "Divorce isn't exactly an option in this pack."

"I see." She frowns, her forehead creasing in thought.

"Whatever you're imagining, I can promise you it's worse," I say quietly.

"What about Mia and Ramsey's dads? Are they married?"

"Charlie and Anthony are both single. Mia's mom died from an illness when Mia was young," I explain. "As far as I know, Charlie hasn't even dated since."

"And Ramsey's dad?"

"Anthony's wife Kim was killed several years ago."

"Killed by who?" she asks. And then in a lowered voice, "Franco?"

"No," I say grimly. Again, I don't bother sugarcoating it. Anyone listening already knows. "Anthony found out she was having an affair."

"That's awful." She swallows hard, and I wait, wondering if she's heard enough. But then she clears her throat. "And the women behind Franco's generals?" she asks. "Are they generals' wives too?"

"Yeah, the brunette, Gina, is married to Conrad," I say. "The blonde beside her is Andy. She's Toros's new wife."

"She looks my age," Lexi murmurs.

I don't correct her. The truth is Andy is barely twenty years old. I've never spoken to her, and I can only hope she chose her marriage willingly—a valid concern considering her groom is a mafia general twice her age.

The room finally begins to fill up as various lieutenants and other leaders join us.

Meetings like these are designed to include the generals' regimes, to give them a glimpse into what they're a part of. Franco says it inspires community and loyalty, but I know what he really uses this gathering for. Fear. It's his favorite motivator and one I've seen both him and my father wield like a weapon whether we're in a boardroom or a brawl.

I notice the moment Franco walks into the room.

My eyes are drawn to him like they would be to any predator who's just entered my environment. My blood pumps harder and hotter. My wolf strains against the leash of my human body.

The alpha in me thirsts to spill his blood.

Is this what my father feels all the time? Has the thirst driven him slowly insane after all these years?

Lexi tenses, and I realize she's seen Franco now too.

I reach over to reassure her, but movement in the aisle draws my attention. I look up just as a body drops into the empty seat on Lexi's other side.

"Hello, Jericho." Dominic Albero grins at me, a flash of white teeth that's more snarl than polite greeting. He doesn't wait for me to say a word before turning to Lexi. "Hello, beautiful. Is this seat taken?"

15

LEXI

Words stick in my throat as Dom makes himself comfortable beside me. His suit is spotless, his cologne so thick it clogs my throat. He angles himself so that he's leaning his arm against mine. For a second, I'm too surprised and terrified to react. Ramsey warned me Dom would find me. But is he stupid enough to ask me for information right here in front of Grey and Vincenzo? I'd never make it out of this room alive.

Maybe that's his goal.

But he doesn't bring it up as he adjusts his legs so that his thigh brushes mine.

I flinch, scooting toward Grey.

Dom grins, clearly enjoying my discomfort, but the movement of his cheek makes the scratch on it more noticeable, and I can't help smirking at the sight of it, despite my fear. I love that I managed to inflict damage he's forced to see in the mirror.

"Relax," he says. "I'm only here to offer moral support. These meetings can be a bit overwhelming at first." He leans in, adding, "Although, I'm sure you've seen some shit in your line of work, huh?"

He's trying to bait me. Rather than give him the satisfaction, I toss back, "I've definitely seen scum like you."

"Funny," he says. "But I can guarantee you've never met a man like me."

I suppress a shudder at the undertone. Grey presses in closer to me, his body rigid as he leans forward to glare at Dom. "What the fuck do you want, Albero?" he asks in a low voice.

Around us, the room is starting to quiet. People are taking their seats. Security's pulling the doors shut, sealing us in.

"I already told you, just offering moral support for her first time." He chuckles. "A girl never forgets her first, and today's going to be extra eventful."

"Fuck off," Grey warns him.

Dom's eyes rake over me, leaving a trail of disgust across my skin. "Believe me, fucking is top of my list."

Grey snarls and starts to reply, but he stops as someone else joins our row. A flash of red hair catches my eye, and I look up to see Mia dropping into the seat on Dom's other side.

Her smile is warm enough, but her eyes are ice cold. "Dom, he's let you out of your cage, I see."

Dom turns to her smoothly. "Mia Reyes, the equal opportunity general-in-waiting, all the way up here in the back row." He *tsk*s and adds, "How will you ever keep hold of your daddy's coattails sitting so far away from him?"

Mia bats her lashes. "Funny. I was just wondering how you keep your nose so firmly in Franco's asshole from way up here."

Dom's friendly façade drops away. "Watch your fucking mouth, bitch."

Mia simply smiles back at him. Then she glances past Dom and shoots me a wink before settling back in her seat, unruffled in the face of his anger. Seriously impressive.

Grey, however, is practically vibrating with rage. And Dom knows it.

"I'm surprised your alpha allowed you to attend this meeting," Dom remarks. He doesn't look at Grey, but I know that's who he's talking to. "Considering you betrayed him the last time you were here. But then, I guess he's forgiven you since you brought him a consolation prize." He looks pointedly at me.

"I'm not a fucking trophy," I tell him.

"A peace offering then." Dom shrugs. "How did Vincenzo react when he found out you tried to join our side?" he goes on. "Probably not well."

"Shut the fuck up, Albero." Grey's voice is brittle and clipped.

One glance at him, and I can see he's hanging onto his control by a thread. It's tempting to let him lose it. Dom deserves whatever Grey would do. But not here in a room full of generals who'd condemn Grey for what would probably look like an unprovoked attack.

The thought of Vincenzo punishing Grey again isn't a welcome one.

I grab Grey's hand and squeeze.

"From what I hear, Grey's return to the family was met with celebration," I say before Grey can say something he can't take back. "They never did get to congratulate him on killing your brother."

"Ouch," Mia says with utter sarcasm.

Dom's face flushes as he glares at me. He doesn't say a word for a long moment, and I can tell I've surprised him. I'm not sure if he didn't expect me to talk shit or didn't realize Grey would've told me what really happened.

Either way, I smirk at the obvious direct hit I've landed.

At the podium down front, Franco stands up and calls the meeting to order. Dom goes quiet though he doesn't leave. I keep my attention on him so I can be ready if he tries to pull anything, but I also can't help watching Franco. He looks completely at ease in this room full of mafia monsters, all of whom rule this city like some kind of celebrity killers.

"Good morning, gentlemen," Franco says. "Thank you for coming."

Ironic since they undoubtedly had no choice.

"As is our monthly custom, we've gathered today in a show of peace and goodwill among our pack and its leadership." He glances at Vincenzo, and I swear his lip curls up in disgust before he goes on. "For fifty years, I've ruled as alpha of this great city, and you've all served me loyally in return."

Another ironic statement. Loyalty must be earned, not forced. But I guess no one told him that.

"It's because of that loyalty that we've prospered and grown strong as a community." He pauses, and some murmuring reaches me from the front few rows. "But there are some who've become dissatisfied with their current position. They want more. And they're willing to step on their brothers if that's what it takes. They want to betray and backstab their way to the top. And ultimately, they want my seat."

The murmurs get louder.

Worried, I glance down at Vincenzo in the front row, but he's not moving or speaking. His shoulders are stiff and straight. Beside him, Alvaro is equally still.

When I glance back at Franco, I find him staring up at Grey.

Dread slams into me.

Does he already know our plans? He must know something, or he wouldn't have asked me to spy. Then I realize Ramsey's likely already fed him something and that he's chosen this moment to call it out—in a room full of men who would happily bay for someone's blood if it meant saving their own skin.

"This kind of unchecked greed is a blight on our pack's legacy and must be dealt with swiftly and strongly," Franco says.

The room is completely silent.

My thoughts race. What can I possibly do if Grey's singled out?

"Anthony Greco, come forward," Franco calls.

"What the fuck?" Grey says, and for a moment, I think he's going to get out of his seat.

"Careful, Jericho," Dom warns. "You go to battle for that asshole, and you'll end up on the chopping block too."

"What the fuck is this?" Mia hisses.

From the second row, Ramsey's dad gets up and makes his way to the stage where Franco waits. When he gets there and turns around, his face has flushed bright red. He glares back at the crowd, eyes narrowed on Franco's generals.

"Anthony, do you have anything to say about the charges against you?" Franco asks.

I watch, wide-eyed and frozen, trying to understand why this is happening. Is Franco fucking with Ramsey and me? Because the only traitors I know of in this room are us. Yet none of Vincenzo's generals have said a word in Anthony's defense.

"I've done nothing against your leadership," Anthony says tightly. "These are all lies."

Franco reaches into his jacket pocket. Anthony tenses, but Franco pulls out a piece of folded paper. With obvious fanfare, he unfolds it and holds it up.

"This is a bank receipt with your name on it, isn't it?" Franco asks.

Anthony looks at the receipt and pales. He doesn't answer, but Franco turns to the crowd as if the man's silence is admission enough.

"This receipt shows a significant transfer of money from the city treasurer's office…to you."

A few gasps and murmurs go up.

Grey makes a sound of fury. I grab his hand, willing him to be quiet.

Anthony looks at Vincenzo, but the alpha doesn't say a word.

"This is so fucked up," Grey says through clenched teeth. "That money went to the Giovanni Foundation, and Franco fucking knows it. This is a setup."

Dom's smile slips, and he looks sharply at Grey. "What the hell makes you say that?"

Grey levels a look at him. "Call it a hunch."

Dom scowls.

"Anthony," Franco prompts, "considering you recently gained a seat on the city council—which provides direct access to the treasurer's books—would you care to respond to this receipt?"

"I suggest you start by asking the treasurer himself," Anthony snaps. He glares at one of Franco's generals watching from the second row. "Conrad? What the fuck is this bullshit you're trying to pull?"

"I've complied with all regulatory requests for the audit Franco ordered on my office," Conrad says. "Any discrepancies were investigated by a third-party agency."

"What agency?" Anthony demands. "Give me the name." His face is even redder than before, which is a feat in itself.

"That information's sealed to protect bias," Franco says. "And for their safety." He looks at Vincenzo pointedly before nudging Anthony roughly. "That money was earmarked for schools. You stole from children so you could take more than the fair share given to you."

"I didn't fucking do this," Anthony says, but Franco ignores him.

"This city gave you a home," Franco says. "A family. Brothers. Not to mention the kind of money and power most people fucking dream about. And you used it to steal. To betray your brothers. And to implicate me in the process."

"I told you, it's not what it looks like," Anthony stutters. He's indignant but also clearly terrified. There's no way to disprove Franco's accusations, and he knows it.

Even I know it.

Shit.

This is going to be very bad.

I glance at Ramsey. I'm only able to make out his profile from this angle, but I can see that he's glued to the sight of his father standing on the dais. His skin is so pale it's slightly green, and he doesn't even appear to be breathing.

"We are only as strong as our weakest member," Franco declares.

He folds and pockets the receipt. This time, after reaching into his coat, he comes away holding a gun and aims it right at Anthony's head.

"Fuck," Grey growls.

"Grey," Mia hisses, leaning forward in her seat, "what does he think he's doing?"

"He's taking out the trash." Dom grins just as the gun goes off.

Anthony falls face-first, blood and brain matter coating the back of his head.

Someone screams, the sound muffled in my ears after the loud shot.

"No," Ramsey roars, leaping from his seat and rushing for the stage. Rocco and Charlie manage to grab him by the shoulders, hauling him back.

Another scream.

Then Grey is touching me, pulling my face toward his so that my eyes are forced to focus on him rather than the dead general, whose brains are now located outside his body.

"Lexi," Grey says, his voice far away. "Lexi."

He squeezes my cheeks with his hands until the sensation brings me back to myself.

"Lexi." This time, his tone is sharp and almost unkind.

I blink.

"Stop screaming," he says, his dark, enigmatic eyes anchoring me.

"I wasn't—" I frown. My throat is raw. Another scream builds, but I manage to swallow it.

"Good." He doesn't let me go or look away.

Not even when Franco starts talking again. "This is what happens to those who forget their place."

His words make me flinch, but I don't look away from Grey. I grip his wrists, hoping that means he'll hold on to me too. It's a connection I desperately need right now.

"Don't forget this," Franco warns in a booming voice. "Betray me, and this is how it will end. This meeting's adjourned."

He drops the mic, the thud echoing harshly. He's speaking again, but the words don't carry this far without the microphone.

Clothes rustle as people rise and begin to move. The hum of voices fills my ears.

"We're leaving now," Grey says to me. "Okay?"

"Okay," I manage.

He finally releases my face and wraps his hand around mine, holding tight. "Stand up."

I do as he says, glad for the instruction and even more relieved my body knows to obey. I'm not sure it would listen to me right now.

When I stand and turn for the aisle, I find Mia waiting for me there. Dom is gone. I don't look for him.

"Come here," Mia says, holding out her hand.

I grasp her hand with my free one and let her lead me down the center aisle steps. My heart thuds as we get closer to the ground level—to the dead man lying there—but Mia turns left halfway there and slips out a side door.

A few others with the same idea are just ahead of us in a dark hallway. No one speaks to us. I keep a tight hold of Mia's hand with my left while still squeezing Grey's hand with my right.

We descend a musty stairwell then push out into bright sunshine that's jarring to my panicked senses. It's too bright. Too warm. And entirely too cheerful for what I just witnessed.

My stomach rolls with nausea.

"Here." Mia pulls me over to where Grey's driver holds

the car door open. Before I slip inside, she grabs me by the shoulders and turns me to face her. "Deep breaths. Count to ten. You'll be fine."

I nod, taking her word for it. Then I reluctantly release both their hands and climb into the car.

16

GREY

My wolf's caught between wanting to drive Lexi as far as this car will take us and tearing chunks out of Franco until he's nothing more than blood and bones beside Anthony's body.

Mia must sense my dilemma because she grabs my arm the moment Lexi's ducked inside the car.

"She's the priority," she says firmly. "Do you hear me?"

I don't answer. Adrenaline and rage clog my throat. Vengeance and despair course through me like they're strands of my DNA.

"Grey," Mia snaps.

I scowl at her. "What?"

"Take her to my house. I'll be there soon."

"No." She should go home where I can hold her. Where I can convince her not to run away screaming from this life—from me and everything I am.

"I can call the others," she says. "We'll debrief together

so we can figure out what this means for us. And Lexi will do better with company right now."

I sigh. She's right. We need to get in front of this before my father can organize some kind of rash response. I'm not going to let this city get caught in a war. "Fine. But I need to make a stop first."

"Don't be long." Mia hurries to her waiting car.

I give Elio instructions about our destination before joining Lexi in the car. She's slid all the way to the far side of the seat, and her arms are wrapped around herself. But she's dry-eyed, and she's stopped shaking.

That's a good sign.

The moment the door shuts, I pour her a glass of orange juice from the car's stocked mini fridge and hold it out to her. "Here. The sugar will help your nerves."

She takes it and sips.

I nod at her to do it again.

She empties the glass and hands it back to me. "I'm not going to fall apart." She must see something in my expression because she adds, "Again."

Despite everything, my lips twitch. But my amusement fades quickly. "I'm sorry," I tell her. "I never should've brought you to that meeting."

"You couldn't have known."

"I knew he'd do something dramatic," I say. "After my attack on the restaurant and our public engagement, he had to hit back somehow."

"But Anthony had nothing to do with any of that. Why didn't he go after you directly?"

My head begins to ache. "It's part of the game."

"That makes no freaking sense," she says, frustration leaking out.

I exhale heavily. "Come here."

Before she can move an inch, I scoop her into my arms and settle her on my lap. Part of me wonders if she'll push me away, but she slides her arms around my shoulders and buries her face in my neck.

Her skin against mine feels so damn good.

And even though she's not straddling me—and her body is a lot more covered—I think of that lap dance. The night we met. The way she seduced me. The way I fell for her the moment she told me to sit on that fucking couch and keep my hands to myself.

This time, I break that rule greedily.

With my arms wrapped around her, I rub slow, soothing circles over her back. My palm slides across the fabric of her dress then over the zipper, which I reluctantly leave intact. Sex would only help one of us right now. She needs comfort. And more than anything, I want to be what she needs.

I wind my fingers into her silky hair, gathering fistfuls of it then letting it go again. My chest presses against hers, my skin warming beneath the fabric of my shirt.

Being close to her, smelling her, touching her—it calms my wolf's blood thirst in a way nothing else ever has.

"I'm sorry I screamed," she says finally.

"Don't apologize." I draw her away so I can look into her eyes. "Seriously. You reacted like a normal person who hasn't been desensitized by prolonged exposure to violence. The people who didn't scream are the ones who should be sorry."

She nods then lays her head on my shoulder again, snuggling in against my neck.

I hold her just like that for the duration of the drive, willing to admit this comforts me just as much as it does her.

And I need that comfort now. I thought we'd have more time, but Franco just ruined that idea. We need to move quickly—to become a pack, to strengthen my alpha power enough that I can take on both my father and Franco himself.

There's only one thing I can do.

We pull up outside my apartment, and I ease Lexi off my lap and onto the seat beside me.

"Come on, we need to go." I tug her hand, and we climb out of the car into the sunlight. My apartment building rises in front of us, but I turn away from it to address Elio. "We're on our own from here."

"Sir?"

"I'll take the car. You have the day off."

"I'm not sure the alpha—"

"Feel free to report me. But you're no longer needed." My voice is firm with only the barest hint of alpha power in it.

Elio blinks then nods. "Yes, sir." He steps away from the door and strides off toward the parking garage.

I look back at Lexi. "Want to ride up front this time?"

"Sure."

I round the car and hold the passenger door open for

her. Then I slide into the driver's seat. The engine's still running, so I don't waste any time before easing back into traffic. Elio will have told the other guards I ordered him to let us leave alone, but that doesn't mean they won't try to follow us anyway, especially if they're loyal to my father.

I drive strategically for almost half an hour to make sure we've lost any tails before heading to our destination. Lexi is quiet and contemplative. I try to read her mood, but I can't sense anything more than low anxiety humming off her.

When she finally looks up and notes where we are, her expression turns wary. "What are we doing here?"

"I need to grab something before we head over to meet the others," I tell her. "You want to come inside with me?"

Through the car window, she studies the warehouse. I know she must be thinking about the first time I brought her here. A visit that ended in me killing Trucker, an informant for Franco. After what she just went through, I hate asking her to come into a place that holds nothing but bad memories, but I also have no intention of leaving her out here alone.

"Promise you're not going to kill anyone in there?" she jokes.

I laugh, though it's not funny. "I promise. Come on."

She takes my hand and lets me lead her through the side door we used last time. I flip a switch on the wall to get the lights blinking on overhead. The place looks the same as always—dusty concrete walls, aging and empty.

Forgotten. The perfect off-grid place for our various needs.

The warehouse belongs to Vincenzo Diavolo, but even he's forgotten it.

I stop in front of a narrow door at the end of the passageway. Inside, I find a mop and bucket along with a few random cleaning supplies left over from another era. The bottles of disinfectant shove aside easily, and I feel for the catch along the wall beneath the empty aluminum shelving.

Click.

I pull open the compartment and grab the hard case from its hiding place in the wall. There's a duffel bag behind it, but I don't take that with me. No need to. Yet.

"Nice hiding spot," Lexi says.

I grab her hand, squeezing for emphasis. "If something happens to me, take this bag and follow the instructions inside."

"What?" Her amusement turns to worry.

"The duffel," I say, pointing at it before closing the compartment again. "See this spot here." I grab her hand and position it over the catch along the wall. "This will open the compartment. Got it?"

She shakes her head. "Grey, you're being ridiculous. Nothing's going to happen to you."

"But if it does," I insist.

She studies me, clearly noting my seriousness. "What's in the bag?"

"Instructions," I say again.

"How would I get through the wards?" she asks.

"The less you know, the better. For now. Don't look inside until you're ready to use it, okay?"

She doesn't look convinced, but she says, "Okay."

Shaking off my darkening thoughts, I push the compartment back into place until it clicks shut. Then I step back and close the closet door. "Ready?"

She nods and falls into step with me.

"What's in the box?" she asks.

"The weapon that will finally finish this," I tell her as we exit the warehouse and climb back into the car. "It's time to move on to the next phase of this war."

Downtown is crowded with a lunchtime rush hour that's busier than usual. I have no doubt word of Anthony's death has already spread through the city. They'll want to gather and gossip and speculate about whether my father will retaliate and how bad the fallout will be. I wish I knew. By the time we pull to a stop in front of Mia's building, I've already gotten texts from both her and Dutch asking where the hell we are.

"I thought we were going to Mia's," Lexi says once we're out of the car.

I glance at the city block of high rises. The first floor houses stores like Les Haut, a high-end clothing boutique. The middle floors are home to a couple of attorneys' offices and a plastic surgeon.

The penthouse, however, has one resident.

"We are," I say.

"I don't understand. Doesn't she live in Pine Hill with Dutch and the others?"

"Not anymore. See that top level?" I ask, pointing.

"Yeah."

"It's a penthouse apartment."

"Mia lives here?" She pauses then adds, "You know what?" She shakes her head, the disbelief disappearing. "I don't even know why I'm surprised. Of course she lives upstairs from her favorite places to shop."

I smirk. "Come on."

We take the elevator up, using the secure code Mia gave us to allow access to her floor—just like my place. The fact that she and I both live in penthouse apartments with top-notch security, however, is where the similarity ends. The doors open to what Dutch describes as a vomit of color. A bright yellow sectional faces a wall of windows, allowing sunlight to saturate the rich hues. A pink ottoman and accent chair complete the sitting area with the throw-pillow-to-person ratio at least six to one. It's cozy and inviting—and bright as fuck.

Lexi slows, taking it all in.

"Wow," she manages, staring up at the art piece Mia keeps telling me is post-modern-something-or-other. It's an abstract splash of bright blues, greens, and yellows, which is basically the decorating scheme of the entire place.

"If you squint, it's not quite so overwhelming," I tell her.

"I heard that," Mia calls, her voice ringing out from around the corner.

She appears a second later, a tray of drinks in her hand. "Stop talking shit about my decorating, Grey. Your namesake's the only color you're capable of using, so you're in no position to talk."

Lexi grins, and I glare at her. "You're taking her side?"

Lexi shrugs. "She's not wrong."

"I never am." Mia softens as she looks at Lexi. "How are you?"

"I'm good," Lexi tells her.

"Everyone's outside," Mia says. "Come on."

We follow her out where Dutch, Razor, and Crow are all sitting at the covered patio table. Mia slides the tray onto the table, and Razor reaches for the bottle of whiskey and starts pouring shots. There's another bottle beside him, but it's empty.

We're clearly late to the party.

"Where's Ramsey?" I ask.

"I sent him to take a shower," Mia says with a huff.

"What? Why?"

"That's why." She nods at the white concrete wall. It's streaked red.

I sniff. Fresh blood. "What the hell happened?"

"He wants Franco's head, dude," Razor says. "Took his rage out on the wall with his fists."

I look from him to the others, my heart aching for Ramsey's loss. Losing his dad is one thing. Watching Anthony get executed like that while all those assholes sat by and let it happen—it's gotta be killing him.

Of course he wants revenge.

So do I.

"We can't let him do something stupid," I say.

"We know," Dutch says.

Mia reaches for one of the shots Razor poured, and there are bloodied gashes on her arm.

My hand whips out, snagging her wrist and turning it so I can get a better look. "What the fuck happened to you?" I ask quietly.

"Ramsey happened," Dutch says.

I look from him to Mia, but she pulls her arm back, dismissing my worry. "Relax, Grey. I'm fine. Ramsey's nothing I can't handle."

"Tell me exactly what happened," I order.

"After the meeting ended, Rocco and my dad helped get Ramsey into my car," Mia explains. "I didn't want him going home alone so I brought him here. He was upset. Obviously. I tried to calm him down. He didn't realize what he was doing. He half-shifted in the freaking car. Almost tore it apart."

I set the box down. "I'm going to talk to him."

"No need," says a clipped male voice.

I look up and find Ramsey striding toward us. His hair's still wet from the shower, and he's wearing a pair of gym shorts. His knuckles are bruised but already healing, from what I can tell. The grief in his eyes, however, is fresh and raw.

"Hey." I grab him in a hug. "I'm sorry."

Ramsey hugs me back hard before letting me go. "The only fucker who's going to be sorry is Franco."

17

LEXI

Ramsey doesn't even look at me as he crowds around the table with the others, shot glasses raised in a toast to Anthony Greco. It's impressive the way he can pretend, even in the midst of such grief, that he's not backstabbing them all. I drink along with them, joining in their somber celebration of life for a man who, as far as I know, didn't do shit worth celebrating. Still, he was Ramsey's father. And I know what it's like not to have one of those. So, I swallow the acid on my tongue and watch them help him grieve.

A few minutes—and shots—later, Mia sits down in the empty chair next to mine. We're set back from the guys, which is a good thing because Razor's re-enacting Ramsey punching the wall while Dutch and Crow attempt to punch each other instead.

Maybe this is part of grieving too?

"So, how are you really doing?" Mia asks me.

Instead of lecturing like a mother hen, she's ignoring the guys' roughhousing, which is evidence that she's not herself today.

"I'm better," I say. "I just needed to get out of there."

She nods. "I get that."

"How did you not lose it?" I ask.

Her eyes are sad. "I lost it a long time ago, honey."

Her words make me think about what Grey said to me in the car earlier. That the ones who didn't scream are the ones who should be sorry. But all I can think is that she has the one thing I don't to keep her safe: a wolf.

The other night out on the highway, I'd been so sure Grey had finally found a way to trigger my wolf. But it didn't work. And now, I can't stop thinking about Ramsey's claims that a single bite would do the trick.

Is Grey keeping that from me for some reason?

Does he really not want me to turn?

The longer I go without answers, the more convinced I am that the only person I can rely on in this city is myself. And in order to do that, I have to find a way to become a wolf.

"Okay, no more shots," Grey announces. "We need clear heads for what we're going to discuss."

"We better be discussing a complete assault and annihilation of Franco Giovanni and anyone he's ever loved," Ramsey snarls.

Everyone falls silent and glances at me.

"What?" I say with a shrug. "Franco never loved me. I agree with Ramsey."

Dutch hoots and bangs his empty shot glass on the

table.

Crow smirks.

"She's got a point," Razor says.

"We're not ready to take him on directly yet," Grey says. "We need to bring more people to our side first."

Ramsey turns to glare at him. "What the fuck? You want to play politics when he just shot my old man in front of the entire pack?"

"What he did to your dad *is* political," Mia says gently.

"I don't give a fuck." Ramsey shoves out of his chair and runs his hand through his wet hair. "I want his blood spilled. We can do this. We *have to* do this." Around the grief, desperation leaks in.

"We all want that—" Dutch begins.

"My dad's gone, which makes me next in line for general," Ramsey interrupts. "I'll have my seat at the table. We can use it to take Franco and Vincenzo down from the inside."

Grey's tone is cautious. "Even if my father names you, he won't talk pack business in front of you. You have to earn the inner circle, Ram. Remember how pissed he was about our attack on Franco's restaurant?"

Ramsey straightens, clearly only more determined. "I'm a fucking Greco," he says. "I have a right to my seat, and I'm going to take it. Vincenzo won't be able to shut me out, and then we'll have access to all the resources we need to take down both alphas once and for all."

"I think we need to be smart," Dutch says cautiously. "Take this slow."

"Fuck slow," Ramsey snaps. "We've been going slow,

and look where it got us. It's time for action."

"Ram, I think you need to take a breath," Razor says.

"Fuck this," Ramsey growls. "I refuse to listen to you guys talk and talk about doing nothing fucking useful. Call me when you're ready to fight."

He stalks off, shoving through the door and disappearing into the apartment.

"I'll go after him," Mia says, starting to rise.

"No." Grey stops her. "Let him go. Give him some time to cool off."

Mia sits down again.

Through the windows, I see Ramsey getting into the elevator.

When the doors close, Grey looks back at us. "We can't just think about how today affects us," Grey says. "My father and the generals will want to respond to what Franco did."

"Good, let them tear each other apart. They'll do the work for us," Mia mutters.

Grey shakes his head, violence flashing in his eyes. "We can't let that happen. The first weapon my father will reach for is Lexi."

"So, we what? Convince him to forgive and forget?" Razor asks, brows raised.

"No." Grey picks up the case he brought from where he'd stashed it on the ground earlier. He sets it on the table and opens it. "Ramsey's right about fighting, which is why I'm going to challenge my father for alpha."

They all look at him, speechless.

Dutch recovers first. "You sure about this?"

"Yes." Grey takes something from inside the case and holds it up.

A knife.

Not just any knife. It's fancy, with jewels embedded in the handle and symbols carved into the steel. It looks old —and deadly.

"Is that what I think it is?" Mia whispers, leaning forward.

Grey nods. "A hex blade. Charmed with the power to bind souls."

"Where the hell did you find it?" Razor asks.

"The Black Moon Pack alpha owed me a favor," Grey says quietly.

"That must've been some favor." Dutch snorts.

"Why didn't you tell us you had this?" Crow asks.

"You know what will happen if we're caught with this," Grey says. "I didn't want to put you at risk unless it was necessary." His mouth tightens. "And I think it is."

"You want us to pledge to you." Mia looks up at him with pure loyalty in her gaze, and I suddenly realize it's a damn good thing Ramsey's not here.

Then I realize it could just as easily out me as a traitor. My heart races. I resist the urge to get up and move away.

Grey glances at me then back at Mia. "It's time. It's the only thing that will make me strong enough."

"If we do this, there's no going back," Dutch warns. "The other alphas will know what you are."

"It's a risk we'll have to take," Grey says.

"You're really going to challenge your dad?" Crow asks.

Grey's expression is pained. "There's no other way."

It dawns on me then—the reality of what he's suggesting. My own fear was so consuming that I'd missed it at first.

He's going to fight and kill his own father.

If Vincenzo doesn't kill him first.

Now, the fear is an iron grip on my heart.

"What about Franco?" Razor asks.

"My father's the biggest threat right now," Grey says. "Especially with the wedding coming up soon. Once I defeat him, I'll have enough power to take on Franco. Besides, we don't have the numbers to take on Franco's pack. And you know they won't just accept me outright. Not without a fight."

"Wait, you're going to fight your dad *and* Franco?" I ask, panic rising inside me.

"You saw what Franco did today," Grey says. "My father will retaliate. There will be war. And innocent people will pay the price. I'm not letting that happen. I'm not letting you get put in the middle either."

"But if you challenge him, even if you win, Franco won't just sit by and do nothing," I say. "There'll be war either way."

"You're right," he says. "But we can't avoid it any longer."

"It was always going to come to a fight," Mia tells me gently.

"I don't want you to worry," Grey adds. "I'm going to make sure you're safe."

Frustration bubbles up in me. They're treating me like

I'm helpless.

I'm so sick of it.

If Grey isn't going to help me access my wolf, I have to find a way to do it myself. And there's only one person who might have the information I need.

"Okay, wait," I say, and all eyes turn to me. "Before you do this pledge and send up some kind of bat signal, I think we should make Vincenzo believe we're on his side. That way, he'll never see your challenge coming." Grey looks ready to argue, so I press on, "You told me what he did last time—sidestepping his own fight at the last minute by nominating a champion. He could easily do that again."

Grey looks at me warily. "What do you have in mind?"

"Well," I say, my thoughts racing to form a plan they'll get behind, one that will give me a chance to get what I need in time. "If he were going to make someone else fight in his place, it would probably be one of his generals, right?"

Dutch shrugs. "My dad would do it in a heartbeat." He glances at Grey apologetically. "No offense."

Grey shakes his head. "None taken."

"Yeah, my old man would too," Razor pipes up reluctantly.

Crow grunts in agreement. He looks at Grey. "She's not wrong. Besides, even if you did fight a champion in his place and win the title, Vincenzo would still be alive. And that makes him a threat."

"Right, so we need to make sure the generals can't step in," I say, warming to my idea. With any luck, they'll all be too distracted to notice I have my own agenda.

Mia looks from me to Grey. "How do we do that?"

I hesitate, waiting to see what Grey will say. My idea might be perfect—or it might piss him off.

"I know a way," he says, and I exhale, relieved at not having to say it.

I listen as he tells the others about the chemical Franco had him use five years ago. Dutch and Mia don't look shocked, but Razor and Crow are clearly hearing this part of the story for the first time.

"Dude, that's so fucked up. Why didn't you tell me?" Razor asks.

"We could've helped you," Crow says quietly, the hurt in his voice unmistakable.

Grey's jaw is stubbornly set. "You saw what my father was willing to do to me—to all of us—for defying him. If he thought you were involved in what I did, you all would've been in danger."

"You don't look surprised," Razor says to Dutch. "You knew."

"Not at the time. I mean, I suspected Grey was up to something, but I didn't have proof. He told me after. When Vincenzo told him to get the hell out of the city. I made sure Vincenzo couldn't track Grey down—just in case he changed his mind about letting him live."

"Fuck," Razor snarls. "That guy deserves everything that's coming to him."

"And you?" Crow asks Mia. "You knew?"

"Not until recently," she says.

Crow looks at Grey. "You told her but not us?"

"No," Mia says. "My dad told me."

Crow's eyes widen. "Why the hell would he do that?"

"I don't know. He's been more forthcoming lately. I figured it was part of his training or passing the torch or whatever." She looks at Grey. "Maybe it's more than that."

"Charlie doesn't approve of everything my father's doing," Grey says. He glances at me. "Especially with Lexi."

That startles me.

I'm not sure how far his disapproval extends, but I tuck it away for later. For now, I stay focused on making this work for me—before it's too late and I'm caught in a war between deadly wolves with no way to protect myself.

"So, you want to give the generals that same drug?" I ask.

Grey shakes his head. "Not the same one, no. My father would suspect me immediately. We need to do something to weaken them, though."

"We could throw a party," I suggest.

"What kind of party?" Mia asks.

I shrug. "Something to do with the wedding maybe? We get all the generals together and push drinks on them. Get them drunk enough that they won't notice if you slip them something else. Leave Vincenzo out of it. Then, at the end of the night, issue your challenge. He'll be the only one fit to fight."

The others are quiet for a moment.

Razor's the first to nod. "It's a good idea. Those assholes would never see it coming."

"I don't know if he'd buy that we want them to celebrate our wedding," Grey says.

Another beat of silence.

"We can call it a celebration of life for Anthony," Crow offers.

Mia nods. "They couldn't say no to that."

"We need a venue," Dutch says. "Somewhere they're comfortable enough to let their guard down."

"And with minimal security," Mia adds.

"What about the suite at the tower?" Razor suggests.

Dutch snaps his fingers. "That could work. I can tap into the security feed and set Crow up with a live stream so he can watch our backs."

"And it's private enough that no one else will bother us," Mia says.

"It's one of the few places they think they're safe," Razor agrees.

"What's the tower?" I ask.

"It's the corporate office for the Diavolo pack-owned businesses. It's the tallest building in the city, so we call it the tower," Mia explains. "All our dads have offices there. But one floor up, there's this huge suite meant for entertaining. Couches, a bar, screens, the whole deal. They like to party up there after hours, so it's already stocked with what we'd need."

"Sounds perfect," I say. "And while you guys are feeding the generals their drinks, I can distract Vincenzo."

"Absolutely not," Grey growls. "You'll be at the penthouse where it's safe."

"I'm not staying behind," I say, bracing myself for an argument.

"Yes, you are." The look on his face is unyielding, but

I'm not taking no for an answer on this one. "My father is dangerous—"

"He doesn't see me as a threat," I cut in. "He'd have to take me seriously to consider me dangerous. To him, I'm a worthless, stupid woman. Something to be used and manipulated. He'll never suspect I'm up to anything."

Grey shakes his head, unconvinced.

I look away from him to the others, searching for an ally.

Mia meets my gaze, nodding. She looks back at Grey. "She's right," Mia tells him. "Vincenzo will spend the entire time reminding her who's really in charge. A bunch of alpha bullshit. It's the perfect distraction."

"I agree," Razor pipes up, earning him a heated glare from Grey.

"No one asked you," Grey grumbles.

"It would split our focus if we leave her at the penthouse," Crow says, the voice of reason. "You'll be distracted all night knowing she's alone. It'll make you sloppy."

"I'm never sloppy," Grey snarls.

Mia rolls her eyes. "We're just going to give you two a couple of minutes to talk this out." She pushes to her feet, nodding at the others to do the same.

"Right." Dutch stands, tapping Razor's shoulder.

Razor and Crow push back from their chairs.

They all head back inside the apartment, closing the door behind them. When we're alone, I try to wait out the silence, but Grey's clearly not going to start the conversation.

"I can do this," I say.

"Absolutely fucking not." Grey's tone is final, but I refuse to give up.

"What happened to being in this equally?" I cross my arms. "You said—"

"I don't care what I said. You don't know how dangerous this world is for someone—" He doesn't finish it, but the damage is done.

My hands ball into fists. "Someone like me."

"Lexi." He sighs but makes no move to correct himself.

I laugh without a single shred of humor. "So, it's okay for you to risk your life, or for the others to risk theirs, but not for me, the weak little human? I thought you said you weren't like your father."

He closes the distance between us, his rage pushing to the surface. "I am nothing like him," he nearly yells.

The storm in his eyes should probably intimidate me. Instead, it makes me want to wrap my arms around him and comfort him. Because it's easy to see what has him falling apart: fear.

Before I can do that, his phone rings.

He yanks it out and answers angrily without even looking at the screen. "What?"

Instantly, his expression changes.

"No, I— What? You texted me this morning," he says, his tone a mixture of confusion and impatience. "You told me to bring her."

He listens to whoever's on the other end then says, "I can screenshot the fucking text if you want, but you—"

He goes silent as he paces along the balcony.

Finally, he says, "I'm not fucking lying."

His teeth are gritted, his expression pinched tight with fury.

"Fine. I'll be there," he says and ends the call.

"Who was that?" I ask.

"My father."

"What—"

He stares down at his phone, mouth set in a hard line. "He's pissed you came to the meeting today. Said we need to be at the funeral but no more public appearances until then."

"What do you mean? I thought he texted you—"

He holds his phone up, showing me the text thread. "The punctuation is missing. I should've fucking known it was a hack. Dammit." He stalks past me toward the door.

"Where are you going?" I ask.

"I need to put Dutch on this," he says. "To trace this text and see if I'm right about who really sent it."

"Who do you think it was?" I ask.

"Dom."

The moment he says it, I realize he's probably right. "Do you think Franco told him to?"

"No. I think he's playing a fucking game all his own." He shakes his head. "Probably getting back at me for that package."

My fear becomes wariness. "What package?"

He sighs. "When I heard he put his hands on you the other night..." Fury twists his features. "I should've done much worse."

"Grey. What package?"

"I sent him a picture of Tio with a pig's heart on top."

I stare at him, stunned. "You killed a pig?"

"No. I had Dutch go to the slaughterhouse and buy one."

I don't know whether to be relieved or disturbed. "Grey."

"Let me talk to Dutch. I'll be right back."

"Wait. Just hear me out. Your dad's pissed you brought me to the meeting because he doesn't want to jeopardize what he sees as his golden ticket, right?" He doesn't answer, but I can see I'm right. "Throw the party," I say. "Invite a bunch of dancers. Booze, drugs, whatever. While they're all distracted, you can slip the generals something. They'll never see it coming. Then, when they're out, you can use the blade and become a pack. By the time you challenge your father, there'll be nothing he can do to get out of it." I take a breath, steadying myself until the words feel true. "This will work. And then it'll all be over."

"Lexi." He exhales, his shoulders sagging. But he doesn't back off. He holds my gaze, pleading with his eyes, and his hand comes up to cup my cheek. It's warm and gentle against my skin. The contact strengthens the buzz of connection I've felt since the other night out on the highway.

I lean into it—into him—and melt when his mouth brushes mine.

"I can't lose you," he whispers.

And even though a shudder of unease tells me it's a lie, I say, "You won't."

18

GREY

Anthony Greco's funeral is a huge affair despite only two days' notice. The church, a non-denominational cathedral smack in the middle of downtown, feels more like a palace paid for with blood than a holy place. Its stained-glass windows and high, painted ceilings remind me that what matters most in this city are appearances. Fitting considering the crowd in attendance is only here to gawk and gossip anyway.

It grates on me, the mourners dressed in black filing past Ramsey and his aunt Sylvia, offering their empty condolences. Half of them never met the man lying lifeless in the casket up front. And even if they did, Anthony wasn't exactly a loved member of the community. They're here for politics. Anthony was a city official, a business owner, and most importantly, a general for the Diavolo family.

If he's gone, there's a power vacuum—or at least, that's what the media's calling it.

Like sharks to blood, they smell the opportunity this presents.

Maybe that's why my father didn't bat an eye when I suggested we hold a party in Anthony's honor at the tower tonight. He needs to show strength right now. Business as usual. Nothing says "I'm not shaken" like getting wasted at your corporate headquarters on a Wednesday night. He hasn't even brought up the text he claims he didn't send or Lexi's attendance at that meeting. It's like our phone call never happened.

In fact, Vincenzo Diavolo is clear-eyed and smiling as he greets the attendees on their way past the casket. His dark suit is spotless, and his eyes have never been drier. The only sign that he's acknowledging the high stakes is the security detail he arrived with. At least six men escorted him inside. They've positioned themselves near where he stands now, trying—and failing—to blend in. Anytime anyone makes a sudden movement, one of them gets up and shoves them back until my father clears the person to pass.

Even Ramsey was blocked from approaching.

Ramsey's prediction that he'll be welcomed as a general was naïve. He spent the last two days drinking himself into oblivion while his aunt Sylvia made the arrangements for today's service. The fact that he couldn't pull himself together hasn't gone unnoticed by the pack leaders.

Tucked into the fourth row, Dutch sits on my left.

Razor and Mia are in the back somewhere, keeping an eye on the room and all the players in it. Crow's on standby at Mia's penthouse in case shit hits the fan. He wouldn't be welcome here, and we can't afford to piss off the generals —not today.

Lexi's on my right. She's quiet, taking it all in. The last two days have been a whirlwind of making plans for this party and talking through all the ways tonight could go wrong.

I hate involving Lexi.

She shouldn't be exposed to any more danger than she already is, but I also can't leave her alone. After hacking the phone company, Dutch traced the IP using cell towers and a bunch of shit I don't understand to prove Dom was the one who texted me, pretending to be my father. He clearly wanted Lexi to witness what happened to Anthony. Or maybe he wanted to show me he could get to her—and me. Either way, I'm not going to let him fuck with her again.

Franco and his people walk in just as the organ begins to play.

The rest of the guests hurry to take their seats, but Franco ambles. There's no other word for it. He makes his way to the front so slowly that the organ's song ends, pauses, then begins again. Dom and the other generals trail him, the former winking at Lexi as he passes our row.

She stiffens beside me, relaxing only a little when he finally turns back to his own people again. They all settle in the front row across the aisle from Ramsey and Sylvia.

In the second row, my father's men look over at Franco's people.

The generals all nod stiffly at one another.

The two alphas don't even make eye contact.

Dom makes it a point to look over at the casket then shake his head as if to say the deceased brought this on himself.

Fucker.

I stare at his profile as if my eyes could burn a hole through his temple. My hands curl into fists as rage courses through me. All I can think about is how he put his hands on Lexi, touched her without her permission—and without mine.

My wolf wants vengeance.

Don't be reckless.

I can practically hear Dutch's voice in my head. It was a hell of a lot easier to agree with that sentiment before he smiled at me while Anthony Greco was shot in the head. Now, I'm not sure I can commit to that kind of self-control.

As if he knows what I'm battling, Dutch bumps his shoulder into mine. I tear my gaze away from Dom and glance at my second. He shakes his head subtly.

I scowl.

On my other side, Lexi covers my fist with her hand, her soft fingers brushing over my knuckles.

Instantly, the contact relaxes me.

My eyes catch on the glittering diamond ring. Underneath it, she still wears the twist tie I gave her. My heart warms at the sight of it. I can't deny that I enjoy the way it marks her. The way my wolf wishes he could mark her. Claim her. At least, this way, the world knows she's mine.

I exhale and look over at her.

In her green-eyed gaze, I find an anchor.

Around us, the organ's song builds, sweeping and sad. In this moment, it feels like a soundtrack to our inevitable end.

We're rushing toward it, faster and faster every day.

The song finishes for a second time.

I look away from Lexi and up to the dais where a robed clergyman stands. He looks somber with his black robe and white hair, but when he begins to preach, it's brimstone and fire. Condemnation for the wickedness that's befallen this family and this city.

It's ballsy considering everyone here knows Franco is the evil he speaks of. But Franco merely nods and murmurs "Amen" in all the right places. The rest of the room echoes his behavior. It's disgusting. The only thing more hypocritical than a remorseless murderer in church is a sanctuary full of them.

I swallow the bile.

The worst part is that I can't really feel sorry for Anthony, only fury and shame for what we've all become. And what we'll all be before it's over. I left this town so it wouldn't break me. Now that I'm back, the only option is to break it instead.

At the end of the service, Lexi finally releases my hand. I feel the absence of her touch like a hole in my heart, but I force myself to focus on the room—on this moment—and whether either side will use it to make a move.

Franco and his people stand, but they don't leave, instead chatting with one another and greeting guests. A quick glance at the back shows Mia and Razor watching closely.

My father makes his way slowly down the main aisle, surrounded by his generals and waylaid every few seconds by those offering condolences. When he disappears into the vestibule behind me, I exhale.

Mia keeps telling me he's not stupid enough to pull some shit out in the open like this, but Franco's never executed a Diavolo general at a board meeting either.

"Let's get going," I say when I'm convinced my father's left.

"I'll get the car." Dutch slips away.

I turn to lead Lexi out using the far aisle by the wall, but Charlie Reyes blocks my path.

"Jericho."

I frown, a little surprised, both that he's speaking to me directly—a rare thing despite him being around for most of my life—and that he's choosing to do it so publicly. "What can I do for you, sir?"

"May I have a word?" His gaze flicks over my shoulder to Lexi, making his message clear. He wants to speak alone.

I open my mouth to refuse him, but Lexi lays her hand on my arm.

"I'm going to wait with Mia," she says, nodding at the back of the room.

"Don't talk to anyone else." I try not to sound

completely paranoid. "Go straight back. Stay with Mia until I return."

"I will," she assures me. Then she slips into the center aisle and makes her way back.

I turn to Charlie. "Where would you like to talk?"

"I think the refreshments are this way." He makes his way up the side aisle before pushing through an unmarked door that leads farther into the church.

I follow, irritated that he's wasting my time with refreshments and bullshit. But the moment I step through the door, he rounds on me, pushing the door shut and wedging it closed with the doorstop on the floor.

"What the fuck?" I demand.

"We don't have much time," he says, suddenly earnest.

"Time for what, Charlie? What is this?"

"If anyone asks, I'm inquiring about Ramsey's mental state so I can report back to the generals."

"His mental state is fucked." Exactly what Charlie's going to be if he's pulling something.

"Yes, I'm aware. Mia's already updated me."

My mind races as I try to catch up to…whatever this is. What else has Mia told him? No. She would never betray me. Maybe my father ordered him to isolate me. Fuck. There are so many reasons he would do that—none of them good.

"Then what do you want?" I demand.

"Vincenzo wants revenge for what Franco did to Anthony."

This gets my attention. Alarm bells ring in my head. For Charlie to admit that…to me…must mean it's bad.

"Do you know what he's planning?" I ask.

"Nothing direct. He knows better than to implicate himself," Charlie says, but his tone makes it clear that's not a good thing.

"What do you know?" I press.

"He'll use the girl. Lexi." Charlie's eyes glitter with the closest thing to regret I've ever seen in a general. It's unnerving coming from any of them, but with Charlie, I don't immediately brush it off as an act.

"Use her how?"

"I don't know the whole story. We've held round-the-clock strategy meetings about how to respond to what happened to Anthony..." Charlie shakes his head. "But your father doesn't attend. He's holed up in his office, taking phone calls."

"From who?"

"A doctor from Franco's past. I don't have a name. All I know is it has something to do with Lexi's wolf. A secret Franco's kept from us all."

"What kind of secret?"

"Lexi is powerful. More powerful than your father or even Franco. Your father wants to control that power. Take it for himself."

I study him, trying to gauge whether he's playing me. "Why are you telling me this? This kind of betrayal will get you killed."

Charlie meets my gaze unflinchingly. "Despite his many faults, your father's always been there for me, but his thirst for power has taken him down a road I can't follow. His desire to own Lexi—to treat her like a possession to be used—crosses a line for me.

"As the father of a strong, smart, capable daughter, I can't sit idly by and watch the women of this pack continue to be overlooked and exploited. They deserve better than that." The steel in his eyes softens for a moment as fear flickers. "They deserve better than us."

Charlie's always been pissed about the sexism against Mia. That's no secret. Even so, I didn't survive in Indigo Hills this long to lower my guard now when it matters most.

"How do I know my father didn't put you up to this?"

"What does he gain by letting me give you this warning?"

I don't know, but that doesn't mean there isn't an angle. "What makes you think I give a shit about Lexi?"

His tone is gentle, but that doesn't soften the blow as he says, "She's your mate, son. I'm not an idiot."

My heart thunders in my chest as my whole body reacts to his words. My wolf strains against my skin, my alpha power surging. It's all I can do not to unleash it on Charlie, but I can't hide the work it takes to regain control.

Fuck. I have no doubt the truth is written in my expression. There's no denying it now. There's also no point in asking if my father knows it too. If Charlie's put it together, the old man surely has.

"When will he make his move?" I ask.

"I don't know. Soon. And when he does, if you haven't made one first, it'll already be too late."

19

LEXI

The center aisle is crowded as I make my way toward the back of the church. Mourners press in around me until I lose sight of Mia. A woman steps into my path, her smile fake, her fur coat real as they come. She extends a hand dripping in diamonds, and I know the only way to get past her is to give her a moment of attention.

"Lexi Giovanni, you are a sight, darling," she drawls.

"Thank you, ma'am."

"Oh, you can call me Joan. Joan Balistrieri. My husband, Fortuna, is your grandfather's attorney. I think that makes us friends, don't you?"

"I—"

"Now, I have to say, the pictures from your engagement party did not do you justice. You are far prettier than those gossiping trollops claimed." She looks me up and down. "You simply must share your designer with me.

The way your curves are so tastefully accentuated… I don't know how they do it."

There are so many backhanded compliments in there that I opt to simply smile in response. Something tells me snapping at this woman wouldn't be smart.

She doesn't seem to mind filling the silence.

"Now, I won't lie and say I was thrilled to hear of your choice of fiancé," she says, not bothering to hide the distaste in her expression. "But you do make a beautiful couple. And what a power duo, eh?"

"Um…" I have no idea what to say to that. "Thank you."

"Grandma, there you are." A beautiful blonde appears, threading her arm through Joan's. "Sorry," she says to me, smiling apologetically. "She got away from me."

"No problem. You're Andy, right?" I remember her from the meeting the other day. Toros's wife.

"Yeah. You're Lexi. It's nice to meet you. Well, nice is probably the wrong word, given the circumstances." She winces at that, but there's no trace of animosity, which surprises me considering she's married to Franco's general. In fact, her friendliness seems genuine and more welcoming than most of the others I've met in this city.

"Your dress is beautiful," I tell her, gesturing to what must be a designer piece the way it fits her.

"Thanks," she says. "I have a thing for clothes. Yours is great too, by the way, and your hair—you have to tell me who you use."

"Oh, you two should have lunch," Joan puts in, her eyes lighting up.

Andy and I share a quick look.

"Maybe another time," Andy says, her smile slipping a little. "Come on, Grandma. We've kept Lexi long enough."

"Of course, darling," Joan tells Andy, patting her arm. And then to me, she says, "Wonderful to meet you."

"You too."

Andy flashes me another smile before tugging the older woman back toward Franco and his men. Joan's fur bounces along in her wake. I'm left with the distinct impression that, despite the older woman's general judginess, I've somehow won her approval, such as it is.

I push through the crowd again, making slow progress.

A couple more people smile and say hello. They look friendly if curious. Some of them offer their congratulations, which is so out of place at a funeral that it takes me a minute to realize they're talking about my engagement. One woman asks if I'll take a picture with her. She gushes about how she can't believe she met me—*the mafia princess*—before her friends pull her away.

Just before I reach the spot where I last saw Mia, another figure steps in front of me and blocks my path. A dark suit, broad shoulders and torso—not another Joan, at least. Still, I'll need to make pleasantries before I can excuse myself. I start to extend my hand and prepare for more small talk when I finally look up and see who's standing before me.

When I do, I freeze, my insides rippling with dread.

"Dom," I manage after peeling my lips apart.

"Hello, beautiful." His smile is cold.

"Don't call me that."

"Would you prefer a pet name? I'm partial to *princess*. Or do you have a stage name you'd like me to use?"

"Fuck you."

"Language, sweetheart." He clicks his tongue, gesturing to the crowded space. "We're in a church after all."

I glance around, hoping for another interruption. People are surrounding us on all sides, but somehow, they seem to know not to bother us. Their conversations swirl, their laughter echoing off the church walls.

Where's Mia? Or Razor? Or Grey? Surely, at any moment, one of them will come along and end this.

"What do you want?" I ask.

"An update," he answers, and my dread turns to ice-cold fear.

"This is *not* the place," I hiss, darting glances around us.

"This is the perfect place," Dom says. "A public event that makes sense for a quick conversation between polite acquaintances." He flashes his teeth in what he probably thinks is a smile. "No one will even question it. Unless you'd rather reconvene in a more intimate setting?"

"I'm not reconvening with you anywhere," I snap.

He lowers his voice. "Careful. Your tone's drawing attention. You wouldn't want to give yourself away here."

I swallow the urge to cough as his overbearing cologne chokes the air from my lungs. He's right. If I cause a scene, it will only raise more questions.

"Now, what do you have for me?" he asks, his tone unmistakably threatening.

I zero in on the thin pink line marring his cheek. It's healed a little, but even so, my lips twist at the fading injury. The one I gave him. "I have nothing for you," I tell him. "Unless you want me to even things up and put a scratch on the other side."

"Watch your fucking mouth," he warns.

When I try to shove past him, he grabs my arm and squeezes until I make a small sound of pain.

"You don't walk away from me unless I say we're done," he growls.

"Do we have a problem?" Mia's voice rings out loud enough that a few of the nearby guests glance over at us.

I'm not sure whether to be relieved or worried that Mia's here to witness this interaction, but at least, Dom releases me. I yank my arm away, taking a full step back. On either side of me, Mia and Dom stare one another down, tension filling the empty space between them.

"No problem at all," he drawls. "You look exceptionally hot today, Mia. Using a funeral to hook an eligible bachelor?"

"You have five seconds to disappear before Grey joins us. After that, I can't promise you'll walk out of here with all your limbs."

"Sexy and mouthy." He grins. "Just the way I like them. When are you going to have dinner with me?"

"Let me pick the place, and we can do it tonight," she says lightly. "I'll make sure the chef seasons your food extra special. In fact, don't plan to live past dessert."

He snorts. "Cute."

A quick glance at me lets me know this isn't over. But he doesn't say anything else before turning away.

Mia speaks up, stopping him. "That's twice now you've put your hands on Lexi without her permission."

A few more guests look over. The conversations closest to us go quiet.

Dom turns back, his smile twisting toward cruelty. "Is that what she told you?" he asks Mia. "That she didn't want it?"

Rage burns in my chest. I want to interject, but Mia glances at me and shakes her head curtly, telling me to be quiet.

"She doesn't have to tell me anything," Mia says. "That scratch on your face speaks volumes."

The crowd murmurs, pressing in closer now. As much as I want to out Dom for being an asshole, this isn't a good thing, the nosy onlookers. It'll cost us—if not with Dom, then with Franco or Vincenzo. There's always a cost in Indigo Hills.

At Mia's words, Dom stalks over to her, pressing into her personal space until the crowd goes still, waiting to see what he'll do. "This scratch is nothing compared to what I'll do to you if—"

"Dominic." Franco's voice rings out sharply in the tense silence.

Dom turns, the scowl on his face smoothing into a cool mask that's almost scarier than his fury. "Yeah, boss?"

"Car's waiting," Franco snaps. "Let's go."

"Sure thing." Dom strides by me then disappears into the vestibule.

When he's gone, Franco remains, his attention fixed on

me. The crowd watches it all unfold. Joan must be giddy with delight at witnessing such drama up close.

Mia steps up beside me, and I'm grateful. Her closeness is a reinforcement I need right now.

"Hello, granddaughter," Franco says finally.

"Hi."

Behind him, Santiago and Conrad catch my eye and dip their heads at me. I look from them to Franco, surprised at their acknowledgment.

A beat of silence passes.

Then Franco grunts and walks away, his generals trailing in his wake.

When they're gone, the crowd returns to their own conversations. I can hear my name buzzing around until Mia grabs my elbow, leading me away from the guests and into a small alcove cut off from the rest of the space.

"What the heck was that about?" she asks me.

"I don't know. He's never acknowledged me as his family before, much less in public."

"Not Franco," she says impatiently. "Although, yeah, that was a new development. I'm talking about Dom. What did he want?"

"He was just being handsy," I admit with real disgust.

"What a scumbag."

"I basically told him that, and when I tried to walk away, he grabbed me."

"Ugh. He's like a toddler who doesn't understand no." Her annoyance flashes toward something deeper, so maybe I'm not the first person she knows who's been subjected to Dom's interest.

"Has he ever…put his hands on you?" I ask.

"What? No." She blows out a breath. "But there are others…"

My stomach sinks. "Someone has to stop him."

"Believe me, he's on my list."

Before I can ask exactly what list that is, Razor walks up.

"Where have you been?" Mia demands.

"Dutch said to keep an eye on the doors while he got the car."

She rolls her eyes. "Where's Grey? Did he finish talking to my father?"

"I haven't seen him," Razor says. "What's he talking to Charlie about?"

"I'm here," Grey says, joining us.

He looks distracted, and for a moment, I worry he heard Dom's comments and followed him outside. But I don't notice any blood or sign of a fight. His suit is spotless and perfectly pressed as always.

"What is it?" he asks when he looks at me.

"Nothing," I say. "I was afraid you ran into Dom."

"Why would you—" One glance at Mia has him narrowing his eyes. "What happened?"

"Nothing worth talking about here," Mia says, ushering us all toward the exit. "Come on. Car's waiting out front."

"What about Ramsey?" Razor asks.

I glance back to see Ramsey and his aunt standing in front of the casket. Her shoulders are bent forward and shaking. Ramsey has one arm wrapped around her in comfort, though his posture is stiff.

"Razor, you stay behind with him," Grey says. "I'll send Dutch back inside to help. Take him home and get him drunk if you can. We don't need him noticing anything off about tonight."

Razor nods then hurries off.

"Come on," Grey says to me and Mia. "You can both tell me everything in the car."

20

GREY

By the time Lexi and Mia finish filling me in on what happened at the church, my knee's bouncing from the adrenaline, and rage is coursing through me. Dom is a distraction I can't afford today, and even though I know he's purposely trying to fuck with my head, it's working. Which makes him a problem I intend to deal with sooner rather than later.

"He's not worth your time." Mia sits across from me in the back of the limo, her arms crossed. Her expression is full of disgust, but her gaze on my jittery leg is wary. I'm running out of patience with this fucker, and she knows it.

"He's not worth the oxygen he's using either," I point out.

She shakes her head. "No argument there."

"Not helpful," Lexi says from beside me.

She hasn't touched me since we got into the car. Her posture is stiff and distant. Dom rattled her.

"Sorry." Mia tilts her head at me. "Hey, what did my dad say to you earlier?"

I hesitate, very aware Elio can hear us. "He wanted to know how Ramsey's doing."

Mia's brows crinkle in confusion. "Yeah, he asked me that too. Weird that he came to you for another answer."

"I think he's just covering his bases." I slide my phone out of my pocket and type a text to her. "He's going to report back to the generals."

When I'm done, instead of sending it, I hold it up so she and Lexi can read it.

Charlie warned me there's something different about Lexi's wolf. My dad wants to use it for himself somehow.

Lexi looks at me questioningly. Mia's eyes widen, but I motion with my hand for her to keep talking. Up front, Elio ignores us, but I'm not taking the chance that he might still be loyal to my father.

"Do you think they'll offer him Anthony's seat?" Mia asks, still talking about Ramsey.

Before I can answer, my phone buzzes with a text. I slide it out of my front jacket pocket and read the message. "It's from Dutch," I tell them. "He and Razor are taking Ramsey and Sylvia home; then they'll meet us at Mia's to get ready for tonight."

Mia nods. "It's for the best that Ram isn't involved. He's a loose cannon right now."

We haven't even told him about our plans for tonight's party. He's been too drunk to comprehend much of anything, and I can't trust him with sensitive information when he's like this. "We'll deal with him after the party," I say, and Mia lets it go.

I glance at Lexi again. She's staring out the window, her brow furrowed in thought. I know she's trying to figure out what Charlie meant about her wolf. So far, Dutch hasn't uncovered anything about what my father's found out, and I can't help thinking everyone else knows something we don't.

"You okay?" I ask her.

Lexi snaps her head back to me. For a split second, fear ripples in her gaze. Then she blinks, and it smooths away. She reaches for my hand. "I'm fine. Why?"

My phone buzzes again. I look down and scan a message from Crow.

Party favors secured. All set for tonight.

"What is it?" Mia asks.

"Crow picked up our party supplies," I say, sliding the phone away and gathering my thoughts about tonight. Needing reassurance, I reach for Lexi, wrapping my arm around her waist and pulling her in close beside me. "Looks like we're a go."

Mia's eyes glitter. "Time to play offense."

I tap my free hand against my knee, impatient to get this done. After what Charlie told me earlier, I'm more determined than ever to challenge my father and put an end to this nightmare, once and for all. After that, I'm going to figure out whatever secret Franco's kept so that Lexi can't ever be manipulated by him again.

Tonight, I claim my father's blood-soaked title for myself.

Then, I'll claim the crown.

21

LEXI

A few hours later, Mia and I get ready together while the guys run out to pick up the drugs they're going to use on the generals and get Crow set up with the monitoring equipment. Under Mia's direction, I change my dress four times.

"Not red. It's too bold," she says, shaking her head. "Vincenzo wants submissive. Ugh, I hate myself for even saying that sentence out loud. Sorry."

"It's fine," I tell her. "You're not wrong. And I want this to work."

"Try the light blue one."

I strip out of the red cocktail dress and shrug into one with a high-necked halter top and flowing skirt that ends just above my knee.

"Perfect," Mia says. "And leave your hair down. It makes you look younger, sweeter."

I try to use her approval as encouragement for my real

mission. But by the time Grey and the others return to pick us up, my heart is pounding. If I don't find a way to get answers tonight, they'll die with Vincenzo.

And I might be stuck as a human forever.

"Ready?" Grey asks as the others climb into the back of the limo we're all taking over.

"I think so," I say. "You?"

He nods. "We've got this." But the glint in his dark eyes tells me he's not so sure.

On the ride over, Dutch pours everyone a shot, and we all raise our glasses. "To the next generation of the mafia pack," he says.

"Cheers to that," Mia says with enthusiasm.

Razor and Crow murmur their agreement, and we all drink.

When we arrive at our destination, I can't help but think this office looks a lot like GV Industries. But Grey's right. It's taller. As if Vincenzo's compensating for being second in any way he can. Other than that, the interior's nearly the same modern design, complete with stark white surfaces and marble floors.

I shiver as we get into the elevator.

"Cold?" Grey asks.

"I'm fine," I say.

He takes my hand, squeezing it once, pressing my rings into my skin—both the gleaming diamond and the twist tie I'm still wearing beneath it. Probably risky considering Vincenzo might see it, but I need the reminder that I'm not truly alone in all this.

"Okay, once the generals go down, I'll challenge my

father, and we'll meet on the roof with the blade," Grey says, reiterating the plan one more time. "Any questions?"

No one asks anything.

"Let's fucking go," Dutch says.

Razor high-fives him.

The doors open into a hallway.

We file out, and Dutch leads the way to the glass double doors just ahead. Through them, I can see the space already filled with guests. I brace myself.

"Showtime," Mia says under her breath.

Dutch pushes the doors open, and the noise from inside the suite spills out. Music—loud and thumping—drowns out the conversations until the room is only a hum of voices. The scent of cigars and cologne hit me next. I press in close to Grey at the sight of two security guards blocking our path. When they see it's us, they back off, but their expressions remain wary and sour.

They're the only ones not joining in the celebration, and I make a mental note to remember they'll be watching me tonight.

Beyond them, the large room is crowded. Vincenzo and his three remaining generals are already here. Rocco and Alvaro are seated on a long, low sectional in the center of the room, hunched over a tray on the coffee table that's covered in white powder. By the window, Vincenzo and Charlie are speaking in low voices. There are at least a dozen other men I don't know, though some I recognize from the pack meeting. Along with half a dozen women in tiny dresses and sequined bralettes.

Mia insisted on picking out the entertainment herself.

She swore every one of these girls is trained in self-defense and loyal to her and Grey. If anything goes wrong, they'll be able to handle themselves, so at least, we're not putting innocent people at risk.

At the sight of us, Vincenzo pauses his conversation, but his stark expression never changes. There's a storm brewing behind his eyes, and for a moment, nerves grip me, making me wonder if he's onto us. But then he turns away again, resuming his conversation, and I remind myself he always looks like that.

It's his resting asshole face.

From his seat on the couch, Rocco twists around and offers a loose grin. "There's my boy," he calls, waving at Dutch to join him in front of the lines he's cutting. "Get over here, and get this party started with me, son."

"That's not my kind of party, old man," Dutch calls out. "How about a drink?"

Rocco groans in disappointment, but the mood is light. Aside from Vincenzo, everyone seems relaxed.

Grey brushes his hand over the small of my back. "I won't be far," he whispers.

I nod as he follows Dutch over to the bar across the room. Razor and Mia drift off as well, joining conversations with various guests, and within seconds, they've integrated themselves into the party.

My turn.

I make my way slowly across the room, stopping to smile and say hello to anyone who speaks to me. They don't say much or linger in conversation—probably wise considering I'm here with the alpha's son.

By the time I reach the window where Vincenzo and Charlie are still locked in conversation, I've managed to snag a club soda. Feigning clumsiness, I start to trip, and the soda spills down Charlie Reyes's shirt.

"Oh! I'm so sorry," I say, wincing. "I am so clumsy. Here, I can get you some napkins..." I pause, looking around helplessly as if napkins might just appear in front of me.

Charlie waves me off. "No, it's fine. I'll be right back." He strides off, peeling his wet shirt off his abdomen as he hurries toward the doors.

When he's gone, I turn to Vincenzo, infusing my voice with what I hope sounds like innocence. "I hope I didn't interrupt anything important."

"You are pathetically human," he says, but the irritation is mild compared to what I know he's capable of.

"I guess I am." I laugh and toss my hair.

His disdain is obvious, but I shove that thought aside and touch him lightly on the arm. "Mr. Diavolo, I know we don't really see eye to eye, but you're going to be my father-in-law, and...well, I was hoping you could help me with something."

"I doubt it," he says.

I bat my lashes. "Please? It probably isn't something he wants me to share, but...I'd love to ask your advice about Grey. Can we talk privately? Just for a minute."

His interest sharpens at the mention of his son, just like I'd hoped it would. "Five minutes," he says grudgingly. "Come on." He pushes through the door and onto the balcony.

I glance behind me to see Dutch passing shots to the generals. Grey catches my eye, frowning deeply. I turn away, slipping outside with Vincenzo and hoping like hell it'll buy them enough time for what they're about to do.

"Well?" Vincenzo prompts impatiently. "What is it?"

I twist my fingers together with a nervousness I don't have to fake. "The truth is I want to be a wolf, and I think your son knows how to make that happen. But he's keeping it from me."

He cocks his head. "I see. And why would Jericho know how to make that happen?"

I keep my expression carefully blank like the clueless girl he thinks I am. "I don't know for sure, but…I think he could bite me… Right?"

His attention is suddenly focused solely on me. There's no question I've hit on something important. "What did my son say to you about this bite—exactly?"

"He didn't tell me any of this himself, and I don't really know who to trust, so I'm not sure what to think." I look up at him through my lashes. "Do you know what I should do?"

His demeanor changes, his eyes flashing with anger and suspicion. "Did Franco tell you this?"

"No, why? Should he have?"

Inside, the roar of laughter draws his attention. Vincenzo watches them with narrowed eyes, but when he speaks again, it's clear his thoughts are far away. "Franco's not nearly as powerful as he wants you to believe," he says in a low voice. "I'm not worried about that feeble bastard.

And you shouldn't count on him either. He doesn't give a shit about you."

His reaction throws me off, and I lose some of my helpless act as I say, "Believe me, I'm not on Franco's side any more than I'm on yours."

His gaze swings back to me, his mouth pinched. "I don't need you to be on my side. I just need you to serve your purpose. Don't forget your fucking place."

He shoves past me and through the balcony door, leaving me alone and empty-handed. Through the window, I see him stalk over to the bar where Grey and the others are still serving up drinks.

I sigh, debating whether to go after him and try again. Before I can decide, Charlie Reyes walks out, joining me on the balcony. He's wearing a fresh shirt and holding a half-empty glass of something dark. His eyes are glazed over, making me wonder if Grey or one of the others made him that drink.

"Hello, Lexi," he says, coming to stand beside me.

"Hi." I eye him warily.

"Where's Ramsey tonight?" he asks.

"Home, I guess. He's not himself."

My answer sounds awkward even to me, but Charlie nods. "He's better off staying away for now."

Through the window, I watch Vincenzo snap something at Grey.

When I turn back to Charlie, he seems to be watching their exchange too, and his expression has clouded. He takes another sip from his glass and sways drunkenly. "What d'you know about a Dr. Severin?"

I can't help blinking in surprise. Not what I'd been expecting. "Nothing." I frown at him. "Why?"

"Oh..." He flails his hand in a wobbling circle. "Not important. Just a name I read in your file."

"My..." I put my hands on his shoulders to steady him. Steady myself. Make him look at me. "I have a file?"

"You sure do." He smiles blearily at me then adds loudly, "Everyone does." I glance through the windows, making sure no one's paying attention. "But yours..." When I look back at him, his eyes on me are clear and focused. Intent. "Yours is the only one locked away. In his office. Downstairs." We stay like that for another moment; then he nods once, almost imperceptibly, and puts his mask of drunkenness back on, reeling away when someone calls his name.

"Charlie!" Alvaro pokes his head out the balcony door. "Get your ass in here. We're doing a fucking toast for Anthony!"

Charlie hurries to join them, his steps zig-zagging, but I stay where I am, my pulse quickening as I think about what he's just said. A file—containing a doctor's name I've never heard of. Whatever Vincenzo knows about me or my wolf, I'm willing to bet it's in that file.

I bite my lip. The fact that this file is in the same building I'm currently standing in isn't lost on me. Nor is the fact that Charlie chose tonight to tell me about it. Grey said Charlie didn't approve of Vincenzo's methods when it came to me. Maybe this is his way of helping to make it right.

I slip back inside and spend the next fifteen minutes

helping Grey and the others pour shots. Judging by the unfocused gazes of every guest here, the drugs have already begun to affect them. Grey's focus intensifies as he continues to work the crowd.

Across the room, the doors are shoved open so wide the security guards step aside to avoid being hit. Ramsey stands in the opening with a lopsided smile. He's wearing a suit, though the tie is crooked and his white shirt is stained. "Did I hear something about a party?"

He saunters into the room, pausing long enough to shake hands with some of the other guests before making his way over to the bar. He stops in front of Grey, his eyes narrowing. "You threw a party for my old man and forgot to invite me?"

"You were invited." Grey flashes a laid-back smile. "Although, you might've been a little inebriated when I told you about it."

Everyone waits, watching to see what Ramsey will say or do. But he just throws his head back and laughs. "Hell yeah, I am," he says and pulls Grey into a hug. "Let's fucking party," Ramsey calls out when they step apart again.

The room cheers, and more shots are poured.

Everyone but me crowds around the bar.

I keep my gaze trained on Vincenzo and Grey as I take a step toward the door. Then another. The two security guards standing at the door glance at me as I pass.

"Just going to get some air," I say, but they ignore me.

Apparently, they only care who enters.

I shove through the doors quickly. No one calls out or stops me, but I hold my breath until I'm out of the room.

In the hallway, I press the button for the elevator and almost immediately hear a voice behind me.

"Hey," Mia calls.

I whirl and see her poking her head out of the door to the suite.

"You scared me." I force a laugh.

"Where are you going?" she asks.

"Um, bathroom." I nod at the restroom just down from where I stand, praying she didn't see me push that button. Or that the little light is now yellow.

"Probably a good idea. It's fucking crazy in here."

Someone yells for Mia. It sounds like Charlie. She rolls her eyes. "See you in there."

Then she's gone. And I'm alone.

The elevator doors open.

I hesitate only a second, glancing at the suite doors. Then I step inside the elevator and press the button for the floor below this one.

22

GREY

At the bar, Ramsey slams down the last of a row of empty shot glasses and howls loudly. The generals crowded around him cheer. They egg him on to do another flight of shots, and he motions for Alvaro to pour. The cheers turn to fist bumps and wagers on how long before Ramsey loses the ability to stand.

At this rate, he's not the only one who will soon be horizontal.

We doled out the drug slowly so it wouldn't be obvious and just kept pouring drink after drink. My dad ended up with a few spiked ones because it was impossible to keep them separate once Mia started making them so fast. But I'm not sorry. Not even if it makes him an easy kill in the end.

He deserves everything he gets.

My father catches my eye and nods toward the master

bedroom. He pushes aside the dancer he's clinging to. I follow him into the empty room, and he slams the door shut behind me.

"What's up?" I ask warily.

He may not be as drugged as the others, but he's drunk. And that's never a good thing.

"I gave you one fucking job, and you've screwed it up every chance you get."

My hands ball into fists, my temper flaring. "What are you talking about?"

"Have you seen this?" He holds up his phone. On the screen is a picture of Lexi and Dom standing very close together inside the church this morning. I grab the phone and scroll, skimming the article below. It says the couple seemed "familiar to the point of intimate" and speculates the shared moment was "a lovers' quarrel."

I look up at my father, trying to keep my control. "This is a lie. He assaulted her."

"I don't give a fuck!"

I step back as he lurches at me, getting in my face.

"You were supposed to control her," he snarls. "She's been running her mouth to me all night. And now this." He waves his phone.

"She's not—"

"Anthony was targeted because of that shit you pulled at the restaurant," he growls. "Don't think I've forgotten that."

"Anthony was targeted because of you," I say, temper rushing through me unchecked. "You used Lexi as bait against Franco, and he fired back—literally. He's not going to stop coming for you until he's done the same thing to you as he did to Anthony."

"You have one job," he goes on, ignoring my comments. "One way to repay me for stabbing me in the back: Marry that bitch, and force her to relinquish her title as alpha heir. And you can't even do that without fucking it up."

"You make it sound so simple," I snap.

"It is simple."

"It's not," I nearly yell.

"Why? Because she's your mate?"

His words slice right through my growing temper. I don't respond, but my silence might as well be an admission of guilt.

"Don't bother trying to deny it," he warns. "You think I can't sense it? I'm your fucking alpha. Don't forget that."

It takes everything in me not to contradict him on the last part. He might be an alpha, but he's not mine anymore.

"Why haven't you bitten her, anyway? That's the part I can't figure out. I mean, I wouldn't want the enemy's spawn for a mate, but you seem into her."

"She doesn't know," I say, my wolf straining to react to his insult.

"Yeah, she made that clear earlier."

My eyes narrow at the way he says the words. Like they've shared secrets or something. "You know a bite isn't guaranteed," I say. "I refuse to risk her life that way."

"Her chances are a hell of a lot higher if her mate's the one that turns her."

"I'm not talking about this with you," I say, and he laughs harshly, sending a ripple of unease down my spine.

"Fine, but just know that, if you don't do what has to be done, I will."

"Stay away from her," I snarl, but he merely grins. "No matter what you think of her, we have a code about mates. You can't hurt her."

His laughter dies, and his eyes glitter with hatred. "You broke the code when you tried to have me killed. There are no more rules between us except the life debt you owe me. You'll get nothing from me when this is over. Not even your birthright."

I stare at him, stunned, though I'm not sure why. Even though he's never said the words aloud, I'd assumed it. "You're not going to name me your heir."

"You tried to have me killed," he snaps. "In what world would I possibly name you my heir?"

I don't answer.

My thoughts are a mess. It shouldn't matter, considering what I plan to do to him in the morning. But I guess knowing my father is such an asshole will never stop sucking.

"That title doesn't mean shit as long as Franco's alive," I point out. "He'll just turn around and name Dom or someone else the heir, and then this is all for nothing."

"He won't." The certainty in my father's voice sets me on edge. "Once her wolf is triggered, I'll be unstoppable," he goes on. "You leave Franco to me." More than certainty, there's a smugness to his words that disturbs me.

I don't say anything.

What does Lexi's wolf being triggered have to do with his strength?

"And take care of this bullshit with Albero. I have bigger problems to deal with than a salty second."

"I'll handle Dom," I manage.

He looms over me, curling his lip as if I disgust him. "You fucking better."

My heart thuds wildly as I realize we're actually alone. No security. No protection. I could challenge him. Shift right here and rip his throat out before anyone could come through that door.

I could end this.

For a split second, I picture his blood running crimson over the cream carpet. Coating my face and hands. Seeping into my skin. I imagine carrying the weight of his lost life on my shoulders forever.

My hesitation costs me.

With a grunt, he shoves past me, stalking out.

I return to the suite just as Ramsey falls over, unconscious. The guys pouring the shots all laugh and high-five, but no one moves to help him. I nod at Mia, who hurries over to drag him into a chair. Ramsey wakes up, barely, and Mia holds a water bottle to his lips, fussing at him to get his shit together.

Rocco and Alvaro are back on the couch, taking turns snorting lines. They each have a woman pressed against them, whispering things I'm pretty sure I don't want to hear. Charlie's passed out in a chair by the window. There's a blanket tossed over him I can only assume came from Mia.

In the opposite corner, my father sits at the poker table where Razor and a couple of lieutenants are already in a game.

"Deal me in," my father snaps.

Everyone else folds immediately, and Razor begins collecting and shuffling cards for a new hand.

I scan the room for Lexi, but I don't see her.

"Have you seen Lexi?" I ask the others.

"She went to the bathroom, but that was a while ago," Mia says without looking up from the drink she's pouring.

Frowning, I stride to the door and stop in front of the two security guards. "Have you seen my fiancée?"

"Went to get some air," one of them tells me.

Air? What the fuck?

My temper flares, but I shove it down, trying to keep my voice even so no one else notices she's gone. Especially my father. "You let her go alone?" I demand.

The guards exchange a look; then the first one shrugs. "No one told us not to."

I bite back an angry reply and shove through the doors. The moment I'm out of their earshot, I call Crow.

He picks up immediately. "She took the elevator down."

My heart pounds. "What floor?"

"Not sure."

"Fuck."

I end the call and race to the elevator, slamming the button down hard. Scenarios run through my mind, each one worse than the last. Whatever made Lexi leave the party without telling me can't be good. I just hope I'm not too late to stop it.

23

LEXI

The elevators open to a dark office space lit only by soft security lights along the floor. A small foyer leads to rows and rows of cubicles with walkways between them. I start forward, cutting a path straight through to the far end. Something tells me Vincenzo's office won't be anywhere near his employees. He'll have a corner or some other coveted space, probably with lots of windows and an impressive view.

In the silence, my breath sounds loud in my ears, and my heart thuds so hard my chest hurts. But I force myself onward. If Grey challenges Vincenzo, tonight might be my last chance to learn what's in that file.

I clutch my phone. It's not exactly going to help if I'm caught here, but the camera might come in handy with the files. Besides, it gives me the illusion that I'm not completely on my own.

At the end of the row, the cubicles disappear, and

walls close in. On my right, a glass-walled conference room sits empty and dark. On impulse, I turn left and pad silently down the carpeted hallway. Glass doors lead to plush offices with the expected windows and, yes, gorgeous views of the city. Each office has a name etched into the glass. I don't recognize any of the names at first, but then one of them jumps out at me, and I stop to stare at it.

Dominic Albero, VP of Operations.

I blink, glancing past the name and into the office with sudden panic. When I find it empty, I exhale. Stupid. Of course he's not here. It's almost midnight.

I resume my journey down what feels like an endless hall. The offices get bigger and farther apart until I finally come to a corner office larger than any motel room or apartment I've ever lived in.

Vincenzo Diavolo, CEO.

With shaking hands, I pull the door open and step inside.

The security lights don't extend this far, but I know better than to turn on any lights. I force myself to stand still and wait for my eyes to adjust before crossing to a large desk near the floor-length windows. I spot a pile of papers and a closed laptop but dismiss them both. Charlie said the files were locked away.

I try the desk drawers, but they're all unlocked. Turning away, I study the credenza beneath the windows. I bend down and pull on the drawer.

Locked.

Bingo.

With quick movements, I turn back to the desk and search the drawers for a key.

A muffled sound stops me. Holding my breath, I listen, trying to identify what I heard. But there's only silence.

Then a figure appears just outside the office, silhouetted in the uncertain light. For a moment, my heart stutters, but then his height and broad shoulders bring a sigh of relief.

Grey.

I come around the desk as he enters the darkened room. "I'm sorry. I know it was stupid, but Charlie said there's a file on me, and I had to know—"

He steps into the moonlight, and it's not Grey at all.

"Dom," I gasp.

Before I can even think about running, he grabs my wrist, squeezing to the point of pain. "Hello, beautiful. What a coincidence, finding you here."

"Let me go," I say, willing my voice not to give away my fear. But it's impossible not to notice how alone we are.

"Not a fucking chance, little mouse." Dom's eyes gleam like two cruel stars in the darkness.

I struggle against his grip, but all it does is make him squeeze harder. The pain elicits a sharp cry from me, but he doesn't yield.

I stop struggling to glare at him. "If Grey finds you here—"

His eyes narrow. "That prick doesn't scare me."

My suspicion edges toward fear. "If you hurt him—"

"Relax, princess. You're the one I came to see."

"How did you find me here?" I demand.

His smile is twisted as he snatches my phone out of my hand and slides the back cover off. He picks at it then holds something up between his finger and thumb. It looks like some kind of plastic tag.

Disbelief quickly turns to horror, and my mouth falls open. "When did you put a tracker on me?"

"At the restaurant when you made your little promise to Franco." He tosses the phone across the room where it lands on the carpet, well out of reach.

My stomach churns. "You've been following me since that night?"

"You aren't holding up your end of the bargain. We needed to have a private conversation." He licks his lips, and fear grips me as I realize how trapped I really am right now.

When he backs me against the wall, I draw on every reserve of courage I can find to keep from losing my control. His free hand runs over my hip, and he leans down, breathing me in.

"What do you want?" I ask, my voice trembling at what the answer might be.

"Let's start with that information you promised Franco and see where it leads."

Frustration and panic send my thoughts racing for some way out of this. I can't give him anything that will lead to Grey or the others being harmed, but I know he won't let me refuse him.

I have to keep him talking until I can figure out how to get away from him.

"They'll notice that I'm gone any minute now," I say with false bravado. "When they find me, you'll be caught too."

"Nah. They'll think you're into me." He smiles and holds up his phone. On the screen is a headline about us having a lovers' quarrel. Below it is a picture of us at the church with his hand on my arm. Without context, his touch looks almost intimate. My stomach rolls.

"That's not true," I say weakly.

He shrugs. "Not my fault the media likes to spin shit. I tried asking you for an update at the funeral," he reminds me. "You chose to make a scene."

"I didn't choose any of this," I say angrily.

He snorts. "You're more naïve than I thought if you still think that." His amusement vanishes. "Care to tell me why your fiancé is suddenly partying with his old man after years of betrayal?"

I summon a smirk, heart thudding. "It was all a ruse to draw you out. It worked too. You won't walk out of here tonight."

"Bullshit," he snarls, leaning in so close that I flinch. "You have thirty seconds to tell me something to appease the old man. After that, your naivete officially ends, I can promise you." His hand on my hip dips lower, and I force myself not to react.

The way he's touching me scares me more than I want to admit.

"I don't know anything yet," I say.

"Liar." Dom's hand on my hip tightens. "You know something."

Using his other hand, he squeezes my wrist harder than before. The pain is sharp and piercing enough that it will leave a mark. I bite my lip, my eyes watering.

Across the room, my phone buzzes again. For all the good it does me.

"Fine. We think Vincenzo's planning to kill Franco," I say.

"I'm not asking about that prick. I want to know about your boyfriend."

"He has no plans against Franco right now. We have to deal with Vincenzo," I say through gritted teeth. I'm dangerously close to revealing the truth, if only to make the pain stop. "That comes first."

"What's Jericho planning against his old man?"

When I don't answer, he tightens his hold on my arm until there's a *pop*. The pain sends black spots dancing in front of my eyes. My knees buckle. Now, Dom's grip is the only thing holding me up.

"We're gathering intel," I say, gasping. "Then we'll decide."

"No way. Diavolo would have a plan by now." Dom's anger radiates even through the cloud of pain. He's not going to be satisfied with my half-answers. I try to think through the haze, but the pain is consuming.

"You can't stop him," I say, whimpering. "He's better than you. He's—"

"Shut up!" Dom screams in my face. "Since the moment you showed up, all you've done is ruin shit. You're not worthy of the blood in your veins. You're a failed experiment."

His words don't make sense, but I'm too overwhelmed with pain to care. I bite back a sob. "I'm more worthy… than you."

"Like hell you are. I'm the next alpha of the mafia pack, you bitch," Dom snarls. "Now, tell me what those losers are planning before I break both arms."

Over Dom's shoulder, I see the door shoving open. Dom whirls with me still in his grasp. I yelp in agony, nearly tripping as he yanks me with him.

Grey storms in, his eyes blazing with a fury that makes my knees weak with relief. "Let her go."

"Fuck off, Diavolo," Dom says. "This is between me and the princess." He squeezes my arm again, and something cracks.

I gasp dizziness washes over me and the room tilts.

Grey swings his gaze to me, and his body trembles with rage. "You hurt her." His tone is both an accusation and a deliverance of judgment. He looks at Dom, and his skin ripples in a way I've only seen twice in my life. "I'm going to kill you for that."

In the darkness, Grey crouches, curling in on himself and grunting. More trembles seem to come from deep beneath the surface of his skin. A second later, Grey's clothes shred as he changes into a monstrous wolf.

Dom finally releases me and steps back to face Grey's beast. "She's not worth it, asshole."

Grey growls, low and vicious.

Dom sneers, and he glances at me then back at Grey. "She's spying on you. Did you know that? Informing to Franco himself."

Grey hesitates. His wolfish gaze swings to me, and I can practically hear the question vibrating off him: *Is it true?*

My heart pounds as I try to come up with something to say. "I can explain," I begin, my voice cracking.

Dom's smile is smug as he interrupts me. "Why don't you get back to your party? I'll take care of the bitch when I'm done with her. Free of charge."

Instead of backing off, Grey takes a step toward Dom, his growl louder now. His wild gaze is even more determined.

"Oh please. You fucking touch me, and you're dead, Diavolo." The same smug confidence is still etched into the asshole's expression. Even now, he doesn't think Grey will actually harm him.

Grey doesn't hesitate.

He leaps, closing the distance and sinking his teeth into Dom's throat. Dom cries out, falling back as Grey lands on top of him. The wolf doesn't let up. I press myself against the wall, wide-eyed with shock and disbelief, as Grey's wolf rips Dom's throat out.

Dom's body trembles, his form shifting before hovering awkwardly between beast and man. He gurgles and chokes, blood coating his entire upper body and the floor around him. Then he goes still.

Grey's wolf steps back and studies me with large yellow eyes. Blood coats his mouth and neck. I don't want to look at it but can't make myself look away.

Unlike with Anthony, I don't scream. This time feels different. The blood and violence are shocking, but knowing Dom can never hurt me—or anyone else—again… I can't bring myself to regret what just happened. All I feel is a numb sort of relief.

Then Grey shifts, and the moment he stands before me in his human form, my relief drains away. His glare pierces me straight through my heart.

"Is it true?" he demands.

"It's not that simple. I didn't—"

"Is it true?" he repeats, the words harsh enough that I flinch.

"Yes," I whisper. He snarls, and I rush to explain. "I agreed to spy, but it's not—"

"I can't deal with this shit right now." He turns away from me, grabbing what's left of his clothes. "I'm calling Dutch," he adds. "He'll help us clean things up."

"No need," says a voice from the doorway.

We both look over as Vincenzo appears. Behind him are Alvaro, Rocco, and Charlie. Their hair and clothes are slightly disheveled, but their expressions are intense as they take in the body on the floor and Grey and me standing over it.

Vincenzo glowers at us both. "Your alpha's going to take care of it himself."

24

GREY

My father's wrath is a taste on my tongue. The moment he steps into the room, I tense. Ten minutes ago, I might've put myself between him and Lexi—to protect her—but I can't bring myself to do it now. He doesn't acknowledge either of us as he stalks slowly around the other side of Dom's lifeless, broken body.

My father stares down at the carnage for a long beat. The blood has made a fucking mess; the carpet's beyond ruined. But I'm not sorry. I can't be. Not even if this brings Franco's full power down on my head.

The generals are quiet where they stand blocking the door. I have no idea if Lexi understands that's what they're doing. Nor if she realizes our lives are in their hands. I try to think of something to say, but I'm still reeling from Lexi's betrayal.

I can't think past it.

Past her.

Has she played me all along?

Pretended to care about me so she could destroy me in the end and keep her title for herself?

I don't know what's real anymore.

Or where to go from here.

Help would be nice, but I was too consumed with panic over Lexi to think about calling the others. Now, my phone lies useless at Rocco's feet. He notices me glancing at it and bends down to retrieve it, swiping to light up the screen that's full of notifications, undoubtedly from Dutch and the others asking where I went.

"Boss?" Rocco prompts. "You want me to call the kids in here?"

His gaze is still slightly unfocused, thanks to the drugs we gave him, but he's not completely under the effects. Charlie and Alvaro both seem a little less steady. My father, on the other hand, appears completely sober.

"No." He looks up. Not at Rocco or even at me.

He's looking at Lexi, and the twist of his mouth tells me he's not going to let her just fade into the background on this one.

"What happened here?" he asks.

"Dom attacked—" I start.

"Not you," my father booms at me.

The alpha note to his voice should've closed my mouth against my will. Instead, I go silent by choice. Good to know his power doesn't affect me like it used to, but now's not the time to celebrate it. Or let him know.

"You," my father says, pointing to Lexi. "Explain this."

"Dom approached me at the funeral this morning. He asked to meet us here tonight. Said he wanted to talk about coming to work for us after Grey and I are married."

I stare at her, struck by how smoothly she just lied.

Has she always been that good at deception?

My father's eyes narrow. "Is that so? And what could possibly make Franco's second-in-command change his allegiances so easily after all his years of loyalty?"

"It was a trap," she admits quietly as if she's ashamed she didn't see that before.

My father eats it up. Anything that makes him feel like the smartest guy in the room. I'm a little in awe of Lexi's ability to manipulate him. Has she been doing the same to me? Wrapping me around her finger until I'm too love-struck to notice?

"Of course it was a fucking trap," he snaps, laughing harshly. He looks at me. "I raised you smarter than this."

"Apparently not," I mutter. How much longer can I stand to stay in this room?

With her.

"And did you?" he presses, almost taunting. "Did you get anything important from this piece of shit before you ripped his throat out like he was some common street rat whose death wouldn't be noticed—or come without consequences? Please tell me you got something to make this stupid mistake worth it."

I don't let him see my reaction, but the fury that floods me is nearly as overwhelming as what I felt before my wolf ripped Dominic Albero to shreds. Because yes. I got something very fucking important. Beneath my skin, my beast surges—begging to be free.

For a wild second, I consider letting it loose.

The entire scene plays out in my mind. Just like with Dom, my father's surprise would cost him, and that would be all the opening I'd need to sink my teeth into his flesh and rip it from his bones.

We could be done with this fucked-up game once and for all.

But then the generals would tear me apart, and the only one left standing when the dust settled would be Franco.

I can't let that happen.

Instead, I say, "Dom always thought Franco planned to name him alpha someday, and Lexi being part of Franco's bloodline threatened that future for him. He lured us here tonight so he could kill her. I did what I had to do to protect her."

Vincenzo glances at Lexi's arm, which she's cradling to her chest. He frowns. "What's wrong with your arm?"

She clears her throat. "I think it might be broken."

I ignore the twinge her words bring me. Her pain still affects me even now. That fact only pisses me off more.

"Albero did that?" my father asks.

"Yes," she says.

Vincenzo looks at Rocco. "Do a sweep of the entire building. Make sure this asshole didn't bring any friends."

"Got it, boss," Rocco says and slips out.

"Alvaro, check the security cameras. Verify their story."

After a quick nod, Alvaro leaves too.

Only Charlie remains. I don't look at him. I can't. Not after our conversation earlier. He'll either condemn my actions or condone them. Either way, our moment at the church doesn't make us allies—not for this.

"There'll be a massive shitstorm," Charlie tells my father.

"Should be considered an eye for an eye," he grumbles.

I stare at him, a little surprised, though I probably shouldn't be. He's right. Franco killed Anthony. We killed Dom. They were both generals. It should make us even. But it doesn't. We all know it doesn't.

The rule here is that Franco punishes, and we take it.

Now, I've broken that rule.

The consequence of that is death.

Even through the haze of Lexi's betrayal, I realize this is really fucking bad for me.

"Franco's not going to let this go," Charlie says when the silence stretches.

My father's expression is pinched. He's thinking. Spinning scenarios. I usually don't bother interrupting his ruminations, but tonight, several of those scenarios undoubtedly involve my death.

"What if he doesn't know?" I ask.

My father's head snaps up. He glares at me, but when he doesn't tell me I'm out of line, I press on.

"Franco has no idea Dom came here tonight," I say. "Dom kept it a secret, which means Franco won't be able to track him here. The only people who know Dom is dead or that I'm the one who killed him are in this building. We could keep it that way."

My father studies me. "Did you plan this?" he asks, and I'm too startled by the question to answer right away. "The party. Getting us all together, distracted, drunk."

My gut churns. He's so close to the truth, but I can't let it show on my face. "The party was for Anthony. He deserved to be honored."

"You didn't give a shit about Anthony, so stop pretending you did. The only reason you're even here is to do your job with the asset."

Lexi flinches.

I tell myself to stop caring that he's insulting her.

"I did not plan this," I say through clenched teeth.

"But you knew you'd come here to meet Dom," he says.

"Yes."

"And you failed to mention that earlier this evening when you were watching us pour drinks down our throats."

"Yes."

"That's a direct violation of your pledge of loyalty to your alpha."

And there it is. I brace myself for sentencing. If he tries to beat me like he did at the lake house, my wolf won't let me pretend anymore. I'll have to fight him. Maybe all the generals too. And those drugs are already wearing off.

"You are no longer trustworthy when it comes to maintaining the security of the asset. Charlie, escort her to the estate, and set her up in the guest apartment. Put double guards on her until I arrive."

I blink, blindsided by his mercy. "What?"

He looms over me, clearly misunderstanding my reaction. "I'm taking her, and I don't give a shit that she's your mate, so spare me your empty threats."

Lexi gasps.

My father steps back and snickers, mood changing in an instant. "There. Cat's out of the bag. Was that so hard?"

"Is that true?" Lexi asks me.

Her eyes are wide, and I can't tell if she's just upset that I didn't tell her or if the idea of being my mate is somehow disturbing.

"It was," I say flatly. She reels back like I've struck her. I turn to my father. "Take her wherever you want," I tell him. "I'm going to get cleaned up."

No one stops me as I shove past them and out into the hallway. I don't stop until I'm inside the bathroom two doors down. Even then, I do my best to shut out the weight of it all. I lean against the sink and let my head hang, close my eyes, try to breathe. All that matters is sorting out this mess tonight. I just have to get through this. I can deal with the rest later.

But when I open my eyes and look in the mirror—at the blood coating my chin, my throat, my hands, at the small gash along my arm—I know that Lexi's betrayal isn't something I can just wash off. It's not a cut I can bandage. The wound she inflicted on me is far too deep.

25

LEXI

Fear grips me as I follow Charlie out of the office and back through the rows of cubicles. The lights are still off in the main areas, but the ones above the bank of elevators are lit up brightly. Their glare hurts my eyes, so I keep my head down as I wait beside Mia's father.

Neither of us speaks, but he has to know what I was really doing down there. Then again, maybe he was too drunk to remember what he said to me about the file. Maybe I misread his moment of clarity on that balcony.

Just like I mistook Grey's feelings for me.

Whatever we had before, it's gone. Watching him walk away from me just now, willingly leaving me in his father's hands, was the single worst moment of my life. I don't know what happens next, but I'm acutely aware of how alone I am in this.

Apparently, even being his mate doesn't change things now that he knows what I've done.

Charlie doesn't look at me, but I know he hears me sniffle. The silence feels awkward until the elevator dings and the doors open. Rocco steps out. He grunts at the sight of us, mostly ignoring me and nodding at Charlie.

"You off then?" Rocco asks him.

"Taking her to the estate." Charlie steps into the elevator.

I follow, keeping my distance.

Rocco looks put out. "You got the easy job."

Charlie doesn't answer him.

The doors slide shut.

By the time they reopen in the lobby, I'm shivering. It's not the temperature. Or if it is, I don't feel the cold. I don't feel much of anything, actually.

All this time, Grey knew how to trigger my wolf. Knew that I was his mate.

I find the twist tie beneath the diamond on my finger and rub it absently. I don't know what to think anymore.

I try not to think at all.

Charlie leads me outside to a black SUV waiting at the curb.

He holds open the back passenger door, and I climb in. I half-expect him to get into the back with me, but he shuts my door and sits up front next to the driver.

Then we're off, gliding through the city down empty streets filled with darkened businesses and silent homes.

It's late.

I should be exhausted.

Instead, my heart races with the adrenaline of what I saw and heard tonight. And worse, what will happen next. And not just between Grey and me. He killed Franco's general tonight. If Vincenzo doesn't help hide what Grey did to Dom, Franco will have more than enough reason to destroy us all.

At least, in the end, I didn't betray Grey. No matter what he thinks.

We finally arrive at the Diavolo estate. It's tucked into a back corner of Pine Hill, which doesn't surprise me. Unlike the other homes I've seen in this neighborhood, though, this one is locked down like a fortress. A six-foot wall surrounds the place, complete with a metal gate and an armed guard manning a small booth at the edge of the property.

Our driver speaks to the guard, waves a badge, and then the gate is easing open, and we're driving through the checkpoint. The grounds are mostly thick trees at first, but the woods finally give way to a large lawn before the enormous house rises before us.

The walls are a smooth gray stone lit by orange lights tucked beneath the roof's edge. There are two small balconies with metal railings on the second floor. Maybe it's the matching metal bars on some of the windows, but there's a definite prison vibe about the place. Something tells me every window and door is locked tight and wired with alarms.

We pull to a stop, and the driver lets me out. I follow Charlie to the double front doors and look up at a security camera aimed right at my face.

Everything about this place feels defensive. Like Vincenzo knows his enemies are vast and his days are few.

"This way." Charlie beckons me inside where another security guard has come to greet us.

The armed man barely looks at me as I pass. Is he a shifter like everyone else if he's carrying such a big gun? I hurry to catch up with Charlie as he turns down a hall and exits out a back door.

I follow him into a breezeway that shows me a glimpse of a backyard that looks a lot like Dutch's with a pool and manicured gardens. Then we walk through another door, and I find myself in a small apartment complete with a kitchen and sitting area. There's a bedroom through another door that boasts a small window covered by iron bars. Even with a cursory glance, I can tell the only way in or out of this place is the door we just used.

Charlie leads me into the living room, his gaze sweeping the space as if taking stock.

"This will be your room until further notice," he says. "The kitchen has basic cooking utensils, and there's a closet in the bedroom with extra linens. I'll have some of your things sent over from Grey's apartment, so you'll have clothing and necessities. Meals will be delivered. You can put any other requests on the notepad on the fridge." He pauses as if waiting for me to acknowledge his instructions. When I don't, he walks back to where I stand. "Give me your phone."

"I don't have it." It takes me a moment to remember. "Dom tossed it when…" I shake my head, not wanting to rehash those moments. "It's at the office."

"Just as well. Vincenzo would've confiscated it anyway." He nods at the couch and screen. "The remote is there. You can stream pretty much anything, including music. Vincenzo will stop by when he can, along with a doctor to look at your arm."

He starts for the door.

"Wait!"

He stops, frowning.

"That's it?" I ask.

"Do you have a question?"

My stomach twists with uncertainty. "When can I see Grey?"

"When Vincenzo allows it."

I want to ask so many other things but have a feeling the answers won't be good. "Can I see Mia?"

He softens. It's barely noticeable, but it's there. He shakes his head. "I'm afraid that's not up to me."

"Will you tell her I'm okay? So she doesn't worry."

"I'll tell her."

He pulls open the door and steps out. I catch a quick glimpse of the armed guard standing outside in the breezeway before the door shuts and locks.

The echoing silence that follows hits me harder than I expect. I grab the edge of the couch, sinking onto the cushion as my knees buckle. My breathing is shallow as I struggle to draw in the air I need to stave off the darkness inside me.

I've been alone my whole life but never doubted my ability to survive. I've never wavered in my will to find a way. Being locked in here feels different. Maybe it's knowing that Grey's been lying to me all along. That he never wanted me to trigger my wolf. Maybe never wanted me as a mate at all. Especially now.

The way he acted tonight makes the future feel more uncertain than ever.

It makes me question everything. And that's a prison I'm not sure I can escape.

26

GREY

Rocco and Alvaro find two dead security guards downstairs, but no trace of any other Giovanni pack members. Dom's body is disposed of by Rocco himself. My father forbids a clean-up team, which makes the whole process take much longer than usual, but it means our secret is protected. Or it would be if my father wasn't using it to blackmail and manipulate me into following his orders.

In the back of my mind, guilt for our failed mission tugs at me. I should've been alpha by now, not covering up Dom's murder. But all I can think about as I rip up the bloodied carpet is Lexi.

Her betrayal is a raw wound rubbed with salt.

The others still have no idea.

Rocco makes it a point to tell me he texted Dutch that I'm out of pocket for the next few hours, which means the others are probably losing their fucking minds over what's happening—but they also know better than to show up down here. It's safer for them if they don't.

Alvaro and I carry the ruined carpet down to the dumpster in the parking garage. Then, we head back up to lay the fresh carpet Rocco delivered from some warehouse. I don't even ask where they get the resources they do. It's no longer impressive, just more evidence that these men stay prepared for covering up murder.

When we're finally done, sunrise is just beginning to lighten the skies. I stand and survey the office, looking for any sign of disturbance. The fresh carpet covers the floors, and the rest of the furniture's been put to rights.

It's spotless.

No trace of destruction and death remains.

"Fuck, I'm exhausted," Alvaro grumbles. "Let's get out of here."

Despite his complaint, his eyes are clear and alert. Any trace of the drug we gave him is gone. It's the same with Rocco. Their arrival down here interrupted the slow dosing we had planned, so they were never fully knocked out anyway. I've officially missed my window to challenge my father, and something tells me I won't get another chance like this one.

Maybe Lexi wanted it that way.

The idea that she sabotaged this is almost too much to consider.

The sun's risen by the time I make it back to the penthouse. Rocco gave me my phone an hour ago, but by then, I was too exhausted to look at it. Still, I'm not surprised to see Dutch, Mia, Razor, Crow, and Ramsey all huddled close in the center of the living room. They break apart when they see me.

"What happened tonight?" Mia asks worriedly.

"Did you challenge your dad?" Razor asks.

They scan me like they're looking for signs of injury. I washed off the blood hours ago and put on clothes I had stashed in my car, but I'm sure I smell like death.

"No." I glance at Ramsey, noting that he looks sober for once. "Dom showed up."

"Dom?" Dutch asks incredulously. "How the hell did he know you were there?"

"He put a tracker on Lexi," I say.

"When the fuck did he manage that?" Dutch asks.

"At the restaurant that night with Franco," I say, glancing at Ramsey again.

There's something off about him. His hair is disheveled, his suit wrinkled as hell, but it's more about the way he won't meet my gaze. That, and he doesn't look surprised in the least when I mention a tracker.

"What exactly happened between the two of you?" Dutch asks nervously.

"And where's Lexi?" Mia demands. "Is she okay?"

"She'll be fine." Again, I try to form the words to tell them what Lexi's done, but they won't come. Clearing my throat, I explain, "I noticed Lexi missing, so I went looking for her. I found her in my father's office with Dom holding her captive. From the sound of it, he was demanding to know our plans. When she refused to tell him, he broke her arm."

"Shit," Dutch says.

"We're going to kill that motherfucker," Razor declares.

My voice is flat as I say, "I already did."

"What!" Mia's shriek echoes off the walls.

The others are completely silent. Most likely, they're all playing through the scenarios of how fucked we are now.

"My wolf saw what he did to her, and I snapped." I don't have to explain more than that. Lexi's my mate. I couldn't have stopped myself if I'd wanted to. And I'm not sure how to tell them about the rest of it yet.

"So, we failed," Razor says quietly.

There's no accusation in his voice, but the disappointment registers in all of them. I feel it too, but it's overshadowed by Lexi's deception.

Losing her eclipses everything else.

I blink, trying to shove down the worst of the pain, but it hovers there—backed into a corner and threatening to pounce. If I let it, it'll consume me.

"Wait, my old man texted me to stay away," Dutch says. Worry creases his brow. "Shit. They know something, don't they?"

"My father and the generals walked in right after it happened," I say, trying to focus on the conversation. "Apparently, the silent alarm was triggered right before Dom killed the guards. He and the generals came to check it out and found us standing over the asshole's body."

"Shit," Crow mumbles.

"Is he going to tell Franco?" Ramsey asks.

"No, he agreed to cover it up," I say, studying him.

There's sweat along his brow. I frown. "What's wrong with you?"

He runs a hand through his already wild hair. "I need to tell you something."

The others watch me carefully, clearly aware of something I'm not.

"What?" I ask, impatient.

"Lexi's not... Ugh." He grimaces like he's in pain. "Do you have the hex blade?"

My wolf surges at the same time my muscles tense. "Why?"

Ramsey opens his mouth, but no sound comes out.

Dutch speaks up. "We think he's under compulsion. He's been trying to tell us something about Lexi for a couple of hours now."

Fuck.

What does he know?

And why the hell is he compelled not to tell me?

Whatever he knows, it can't be good.

"Grey, the blade," Razor prompts.

I shake myself, trying to think past the betrayal that twists like a slow-grinding knife in my chest. "The case by the door."

Mia hurries past me and clicks open the case. She returns and hands the blade over to me with something like pity in her eyes.

I unwrap the hex blade and grip the short hilt in my hand. Then I walk over to Ramsey. He holds out his hand, and I see that it's trembling slightly. With a quick movement, I slice across his palm. He winces but stands his ground as blood rises to the surface of the wound.

"Repeat after me," I tell him. "By the power of the blade, I speak truth."

"By the power of the blade, I speak truth," he says, his voice strained.

I press the flat of the blade to his palm so that his blood coats the hexerei symbols etched into the steel.

The symbols glow, and Ramsey suddenly gasps then exhales. He pulls his hand away, bending at the waist as he sucks in deep gulps of air.

I wait, heart pounding.

He said her name.

I need to know why.

"What do you know?" I demand impatiently.

He straightens, an apology written across his face. "A lot of things," he says quietly. "For starters, I know Lexi is a spy for Franco."

The others react with protests and curses.

I stare steadily back at him, fighting the knowing his words bring.

The lie he gave me the night Lexi missed dinner. The way my wolf knew he hadn't fully come clean the next day. I'd chalked it up to his lack of trust. Or him just wanting to look out for me, to make sure I didn't do something rash.

"How do you know that?" I ask when the others stop yelling.

Ramsey squares his shoulders and says, "Because I've been spying too."

27

GREY

My final thread of control snaps. With a roar, I drop the blade and swing my fist at my former friend. Ramsey jumps back just in time, his eyes widening.

"Grey, wait—"

I swing again, this time smashing my fist into his face, and he goes down, landing against the couch cushions before rolling awkwardly to the floor. The others crowd back in again after moving aside.

"Grey, stop," Mia calls, but I ignore her, my heartbeat pounding in my ears.

Reaching down, I roll Ramsey over and slam my fist into his nose. Blood erupts on his face, coating my hand.

"Wait a second," Ramsey yells. He covers his face with his arms, attempting to twist away from me.

He's not even trying to fight back, and that pisses me off more.

"Traitor," I yell at him.

My blood boils. I need an outlet for the fury that's been brewing the last few hours. A proper fight. Not this curled-up bullshit he's giving me.

"Get up," I tell Ramsey, stepping back to give him space.

He continues trying to collect himself but not fast enough. I kick him, and he winces, rolling over in pain.

"Get the fuck up," I say again.

"Give me a minute," Ramsey says, voice muffled now that he's face down on the carpet.

"You have ten seconds," I warn.

"Grey, fucking wait," Razor says. "We need to talk."

"This one's done talking," I say, glowering at Ramsey. "For good."

He looks up at me then, and I can see he's finally starting to realize how serious I am. "Okay, just hang on a fucking minute." He gets to his feet and faces off with me, his bloodied nose staining the lower half of his face. "There's something you need to know. Where's Lexi?"

I was starting to calm down, but her name from his mouth makes that impossible. When I lunge for him again, hands grab at my arms, pulling me back.

Furious, I struggle and strain until Mia steps in front of me, blotting out Ramsey's face.

"Get out of my way," I tell her.

"No," she says firmly. "We need to hear what he has to say. If you still want to kill him afterward, that's your right." Her eyes blaze with fury, and I can see she means it. She's just as upset as I am, but we need to know what information he's fed the enemy. And how badly it hurts us.

Fuck.

"There's nothing he can say that will change what he did," I snarl.

"You're right, but this is about what Franco knows," she says. "About you as an alpha. About our plans. About all of it."

I stop struggling and study her warily. The arms holding me ease their grip. Mia simply waits for me to respond. I glance past her to Ramsey, who's holding his hand to his bloodied nose and scowling.

Grudgingly, I cross my arms. "Talk fast."

"Franco approached me about a year ago," he says slowly. "He wanted information on your dad. I refused at first, but..." He looks away.

"But what?" I prompt. "You couldn't help but betray your own pack?"

His eyes flash. "You weren't fucking here, okay? You ran away and left us to deal with the fucking mess you left behind. So I did what I could do to stop Vincenzo from making our lives worse."

"What the fuck, man?" Dutch says. "We were supposed to be brothers."

"Bullshit. We were barely speaking after Grey left," Ramsey says accusingly. "I stepped up. Did what needed to be done. Franco almost got an assassin into Vincenzo's bedroom because of me."

"Wait. That attack at the estate was you?" Mia asks incredulously.

"What attack?" I demand.

"Last year," she says quietly. "Your mom was the only one home. She managed to hide in the panic room until backup got there."

I look from her back to him. "You almost got my mother killed?" I snarl.

He glares at me, defensive and unyielding. "She wasn't supposed to be there. It was supposed to be the alpha alone."

"Wow, in that case, totally fine," Dutch snaps sarcastically.

"You're fucking dead," Razor says darkly.

"She's fine," Ramsey declares. "She wasn't hurt."

"But she could have been," I yell. "Because of you!"

"I'm sorry," he says, but the sullen look in his eyes says otherwise.

"You're only sorry we found out," Mia says. "Ugh. You disgust me."

"So, you've been pulling strings like some fucking puppet master for a year, and then what? Then Lexi came to town, and you found a fellow rat to team up with," I say, my voice twisting with barely restrained rage.

"What? No." His expression is hard, but his words ring true as he says, "Believe me, Lexi wasn't my first choice, but Franco insisted. Actually, Dom suggested her, come to think of it, but the old man ran with the idea. I had no choice but to bring her in."

I'm glad all over again that I killed Dom tonight. "What did you and Lexi tell Franco?"

"Nothing," he says, shaking his head. "Or nothing that would hurt you."

"Bullshit."

"Look, I fed him stuff about Vincenzo for a while but nothing since you got back."

"Betrayal is betrayal," I say.

He snorts, shaking his head. "That's fucking rich coming from you. I know what you did five years ago, and it's no better than what I'm doing now."

Anger burns in my veins. "I tried to stop a monster who destroys lives," I snap. "I never betrayed any of you."

"You abandoned us for something better. Isn't that just as bad?"

I take a step forward, but Mia stops me. "Let him finish," she says grimly.

Ramsey sighs. "Look, when you got back, I stopped telling them stuff, and Franco got pissed. He compelled me, okay? I didn't have a fucking choice after that."

"And Lexi?" Mia prompts when I don't answer.

"They threatened to kill her if she didn't agree. Matter of fact, she still refused even then. She only finally gave in when they threatened to kill you instead."

Mia looks at me pointedly, but I don't react. I don't know how to feel about what he's saying. It's all too fucking much to process.

Ramsey. Lexi.

It's hard to separate who did what and why anymore.

Even if Lexi was forced, she could've come to me afterward. She could've trusted me.

"Why didn't you try harder to tell us?" Dutch demands.

He's pissed. I hear it in his voice. See it in the way he's trembling, trying to maintain his control. If he loses it, I won't stop him.

"I never meant for it to get this far," Ramsey says. "As soon as I realized something happened tonight, I came clean."

"You're still not saying much as far as I'm concerned," Razor says in a hard voice. His hands are fisted, and I can feel the heat emanating from him.

He wants Ramsey's blood.

So do I.

"You want us to believe you didn't sell us out? Give us something," Crow says with disgust. "Otherwise, you might as well be Franco's fucking lap dog."

Ramsey flinches. "Okay, okay. Last time I was at Franco's place, I overheard Santiago and Conrad talking," Ramsey says quickly. "They said the reason Franco abandoned Lexi to the human world was because his experiment failed."

"What experiment?" I ask.

"Franco has some research lab no one else knows about. Years ago, he experimented on Monte somehow."

"Franco's son?" Crow asks.

Ramsey nods.

"What kind of experiment?" Dutch asks.

Ramsey shrugs. "Something to do with increasing his alpha power. I don't know. It didn't work, I guess, so he decided to try it on the next generation."

"Lexi," Mia says, her voice a mixture of horror and disbelief. "He experimented on her?"

Ramsey nods. "She was a baby, I think. Anyway, when Monte and Carina found out, they took Lexi and ran. Franco hunted them down, but he realized his experiment failed again, which is why he didn't bother to take her in."

"What exactly did he do to her?" I demand.

Ramsey shakes his head. "I don't know. None of it made sense to me at the time, and I honestly didn't see how it could be important if it had failed. But then the other day, I heard Dom complaining to Santiago about the Giovanni super-alpha gene. He said he could never compete as long as the gene was alive. That the only way Franco would ever name him as the heir was if Lexi was gone. Tonight, when I heard you weren't answering your phone, I got worried." He shakes his head. "I'm sorry, dude. I didn't want to keep this from you, but the compulsion—"

"Stop talking," I tell him.

He goes silent, his expression tense.

"A gene," I say, turning it over in my mind. "A way to create a super-alpha…" I look at the others, who all look as mystified as I am. What's in it for Franco if Lexi's the powerful one? Other than securing his bloodline as alpha. It doesn't add up.

I look back at Ramsey. His nose has stopped bleeding, but half his face is stained with blood. The scent of it on the air only feeds my desire to spill more of it.

He's a traitor.

It doesn't matter that he changed his mind when I got here. I can't trust him anymore, and that cuts me almost as deeply as Lexi's betrayal. I've known Ramsey my whole life. We all have. This is so beyond fucked up.

The others are quiet, waiting to hear what I'll do next.

"Look at me," I say, wrapping my hand around Ramsey's throat and holding his gaze. "Who's your alpha?"

"You are," he says with more confusion than conviction.

"Say it," I snap.

He blinks, frowning, but does what I ask. "You, Jericho Grey Diavolo, are my alpha."

"You pledge your loyalty to me?"

"Uh, are you sure you want him in the pack?" Dutch starts.

"I think you need the blade if you're going to pledge officially," Razor says.

I look at Ramsey, ignoring them both. "Just answer the question."

"Yes," he says hoarsely.

"In that case," I say then lean in, whispering the words that will suppress his wolf, just like my father did to me. *"Lupus Muto."*

"What are you doing?" he asks, rearing away from me as his entire body shudders. He looks stricken now, bordering on panic. "Why—"

"Dutch, Razor, get some zip ties from the kitchen drawer," I order without breaking eye contact.

I let him go, and Ramsey backs away, looking past me at the others with mounting fear. "What are you doing?" he demands. "I told you the truth."

"I know," I say because, even if the hex blade hadn't

broken the compulsion, the moment he pledged himself to me as his alpha, my wolf could sense it on him. Even without the full oath, our connection is that strong. But it's not enough to erase what he's done.

"Then why are you doing this?" He keeps moving back until he hits the wall.

Crow crowds in on my other side, probably to make sure he doesn't run for it. Not that there's anywhere for him to go. We'd be on him in a second.

"Because in this pack, we don't tolerate rats," I tell him.

The fear in his eyes burns bright with acceptance. "I didn't hurt you."

"Yeah," I snap, grabbing his shirt and jerking him forward before shoving him down, "you did."

He stumbles, landing hard on his ass. Still, he hasn't tried to fight me. Part of me hopes he will, but if he does, I'll kill him, and I'm not sure I'm ready for that. Not after the night I've had.

Dutch and Razor appear with zip ties in their hands.

"Bind his wrists and ankles," I say, nodding at Ramsey on the ground.

He doesn't even struggle as they bind him.

When they're finished, Mia steps up next to me. She looks down at Ramsey then over at me. I wait, wondering if she's going to advocate for the asshole. For all her shit-talking, she has a huge heart.

"You're dead to me," she tells him viciously. Then she turns away.

"Put him in my room," I say. "Turn music on maximum

volume so he can't hear us. And someone needs to stay with him to guard him."

"I've got it," Crow says, stepping past Dutch and Razor. He grabs Ramsey by his shirt and hauls him up. Then he tosses Ramsey over his shoulder and carries him to the bedroom.

I whirl and head for the fridge, snagging a bottle of water and chugging the entire thing. By the time the bottle is empty, my bedroom door is shut, and music's blaring from inside.

I return to the living room where Razor, Dutch, and Mia are all watching me with concern. For a moment, I think it's about Ramsey's confession.

"Where's Lexi?" Mia asks. "Does your dad know she was spying? Did he do something to her?"

My chest tightens. Ramsey and Lexi's betrayals are a double blow that has me barely hanging on. I don't want to care about either one of them. Still, I ball my hands into fists as I think about her locked up at my dad's estate. "No. He doesn't know. But after what I did to Dom, he's keeping Lexi at his place until the wedding."

"Hell no," Dutch says, shoving off from where he'd leaned against the back of the couch. "I don't care what Franco forced her to do. She can't stay there."

"Dutch is right," Mia says. "Lexi deserves a chance to explain."

The two of them look ready to storm the estate with or without me, so I hold up a hand. "She already confirmed it."

"Wait." Mia blinks. "You knew she was spying already?"

"Dom told me."

No one says anything as my words sink in.

"No wonder you fucking snapped," Razor mutters finally.

Mia looks at me with an intensity that's hard to bear. "She's still your mate," she says. "And she's in danger with him."

"My father wants this wedding to happen, so it's in his best interests to keep her alive."

Mia's eyes widen. "So you're okay with her being locked up there?"

Exhaustion sinks all the way into my bones. I run a hand over my face. "Nothing about this is okay."

"No shit." Razor glances toward the bedroom then back to me. "Do you think Ramsey's story is true? About Franco's experiments?"

"My wolf tells me he's not lying," I say quietly.

"Do you think your dad knows about it?" Mia asks suddenly.

I frown, remembering how weird he was in the suite earlier. And all his questions about Lexi's medical history. "It's possible."

"If Franco experimented on Lexi's wolf, it would explain why he kept her alive," Mia adds.

Franco.

The asshole's been playing me from the beginning. Using me—since day one.

Here I was, looking outside the city for someone who might've helped Lexi's parents escape. Instead, I should've been looking at why they'd run in the first place. The answers were right here inside Indigo Hills all along.

"What are we going to do with him?" Mia asks, jutting her chin toward my bedroom.

"Take him to the warehouse. Make a schedule to keep an eye on him. No one else in or out. No one can know we've broken the compulsion."

"What do we tell your old man?" Razor asks. "You don't think he'll notice a general's son's missing?"

"Charlie knows Ramsey's a fucking mess. He said so at the church," I say. "No way the generals are going to invite him in. Besides, after what happened tonight, they have their hands full with a coverup, so they won't notice if he's not around the next few days."

"What about his aunt Sylvia?" Mia asks. When none of us answer, she says, "I'll go over and tell her he's staying with me for a few days to grieve."

"Thanks," I say, walking around them and dropping to the couch. "Wake me up in a few hours, would you?" My eyes immediately fall shut.

"Grey?" Crow calls softly. "What are you going to do about Lexi?"

The others are silent. I don't bother to open my eyes or face them as I consider his question. I could reject her. Let my father have her and the title when the time comes. But giving Lexi up doesn't stop the corruption. And it doesn't erase what my father's done. What he'll do if I don't stop him.

No matter what Lexi did to me, I can't let my father win.

But that's not what he's asking.

We all know I'm determined to beat *him.* He's asking if I still want *her.*

"Honestly," I say, my insides hollowing as the loss burrows deeper inside me. "I have no fucking clue."

28

LEXI

Maybe it's a lifetime of training myself to sleep in new places, but somehow, I manage to drop into slumber the moment my head hits the pillow in my new home-sweet-prison. When I wake, the sun is high in the sky as it streams through the blinds in the small bedroom. At first, I think the daylight must be what woke me. Then, I hear the unmistakable thud of the front door closing.

I whip myself out of bed and over to the half-open bedroom door. With my hand on the knob and my heart racing, I peer out into the living room. My injured arm rages with pain, but I ignore it as I search the space.

Dressed in a navy suit, Vincenzo stalks through the living room.

When he sees me, he stops—and smiles.

I shudder then steel myself for this visit. Stepping out into the living room, I cradle my arm and stand behind the couch, meeting his harsh gaze head-on. "I don't remember giving you permission to enter."

"I don't remember asking." He sits in the chair opposite where I stand then gestures to the empty couch. "Join me."

It's not a request.

My spine prickles with unease as I round the couch and sit on its edge. Now there's nothing between us but the coffee table. I try not to make my pain obvious because something tells me showing this man any weakness only makes it worse. But he zeroes in on it immediately.

"How's your arm feeling?" he asks.

"Broken," I say flatly.

"The doctor's on his way."

Liar. I don't bother to point out that Charlie promised me a doctor last night.

"If you're here for my grocery list, it's on the fridge," I say.

He tosses a file onto the coffee table. "I'm here to talk about this."

My breath catches at the sight of a manila folder with my name scrawled on the label. "What's that?"

"Don't play games. We both know this is what you were after last night."

I don't answer.

He leans back on the couch, draping his arm over the top. "Go ahead. Read it."

I hesitate, but curiosity wins out over fear. Easing forward, I reach for the file and slide it over to me. When he doesn't yank it away, I flip it open.

On top of the stack is some kind of lab test. I don't understand the list of what was tested, but my name's printed along the top. The date is one year ago. I think back, vaguely remembering an appointment I had for birth control at the free clinic in Lakeland. They took blood...Just routine, they said.

I move it aside and look at the next sheet. More lab tests. More dates that correlate with various doctor appointments in the life I had before coming to Indigo Hills. After flipping through a few, I see that all of them test something called LAG, though I have zero clue what the letters mean.

Anger, fear, suspicion—all the emotions that spin through me as I look at these tests overwhelm me.

"What is all this?" I ask, flipping faster now. Maybe there's something here that will make it all make sense.

Vincenzo just waits, more patient than I've ever seen him.

At the very bottom of the stack is another lab test. The name at the top is different this time. My breath catches. Monte Giovanni.

My dad.

Once again, the tests are all foreign to me, but LAG is at the very top. Beside it, the result reads Negative.

"What is LAG?" I ask, finally looking up at Vincenzo again.

"It's a gene. Discovered in a lab after decades of research on our kind. It stands for Lupin Alpha Gene."

"What does it do?"

"All alphas and their descendants have the gene. It

determines how strong or dominant we are once we come into our power. Years ago, Franco decided to alter the gene for his own gain."

"Alter it how?"

"Successfully mutated, the gene would provide alpha power to a wolf far beyond what we're capable of on our own. Unparalleled physical strength, mental acuity, including stronger compulsion and control over other wolves, even those not in our packs, and anti-aging benefits that border on immortality."

I blink, letting his words sink in. "Are you telling me Franco's immortal?"

He shakes his head. "Not quite. As far as he knows, his experiment failed."

My surprise turns to wariness. Dom used those same words to describe me just last night: a failed experiment. "What does this have to do with me?" I ask, my stomach tightening.

"A few years ago, I hired a hacker to dig up whatever dirt he could on Franco. I expected corruption, money laundering, fraud. What I found was a name—Lexi Ryall. And a huge medical record stored on a secure server at a place called Capo Research Institute, which he traced back to Franco's holdings. The hacker said he'd never seen a firewall like theirs. Took us some time to break in, but eventually, we did."

I gesture to the file between us. "Let me guess: This is what you found?"

"Apparently, every time your name and information were run through a medical testing facility, Franco's private lab flagged it and used the sample to test your LAG gene. So, I started researching what the hell he was looking for, and I uncovered the experiments he did—first on your father and then on you."

"You think he mutated my alpha gene?"

"I don't think; I know. The proof's right there in those tests."

I can't help but feel a little frustrated. I'm finally getting answers, only to be left with more questions. "But I don't even have a wolf. I can't shift. So, obviously, it didn't work."

"You have a wolf," he says so firmly that I find myself wanting to believe him.

Trusting Vincenzo's word feels dangerous, but in this moment, I need him to be right so badly I can taste it. "How do you know?"

"My son senses you as his mate. That wouldn't be possible if you weren't a shifter."

I look away, emotion swirling. My eyes land on the twist tie still wrapped loosely around my finger. My heart squeezes. I look up again, shoving aside the fact that Grey hid it from me. If I think about that, I'll have to think about the secret I kept from him. And how he reacted when he found out. "You make it sound like Franco's experiment didn't really fail."

"Franco assumed the drugs his doctors gave you killed your wolf just like it did with the others he experimented on, so he didn't bother to test for anything besides the LAG. Probably just wanted to further his future research. To try again. But I got curious." He reaches for the file and rifles through the papers. When he finds what he's looking for, he holds it out for me, pointing. "Here. The fever you had as a baby. After antibiotics and all other medicines failed to treat the problem, you received high doses of Aconitumex."

"What is that?"

"Pharmaceutical grade wolfsbane. To a human, it's poison. For a wolf, it suppresses the gene mutation. I think they gave you so much of it that it suppressed your wolf completely. Based on your medical records, Carina gave it to you right before Franco found and killed her and Monte."

My pulse quickens. "Why are you telling me all this?"

"I'm offering you a deal."

My hope is tempered by wariness. Vincenzo doesn't do anything out of kindness. There's always a catch—probably one that will hurt me in the end. "What deal?"

"I'll help you access your wolf. In exchange, you'll go through with the wedding then relinquish your title to me."

"You still want me to marry Grey?" I can't help but ask.

"I want the packs to see us united. To accept me when I take my place as high alpha." Of course he does. This was never about Grey or our happiness.

"Is that all?" I ask.

His expression tightens. "Lastly, you will submit blood samples so my researchers can access the gene code in your DNA."

"You want the gene for yourself," I realize.

Of course he does. If it's as powerful as he says, there's

no way he would let that opportunity go. It's probably the only reason he hasn't killed me yet.

"Franco's time is over. I intend to rule this pack," he says, his expression hardening.

I hesitate. If he has this LAG gene and the power that goes with it, he'll be unstoppable. "What if I say no?"

"I can take it by force," he says, giving me a glimpse of what waits for me if I refuse him.

"Then why bother asking?"

"Why not?" He shrugs, completely confident. "For once, our interests align. You want to access your wolf. And you have no business trying to rule this city. You get everything you want, and no one gets hurt."

He has me right up until that last part. Of course people will get hurt. He can't possibly think I trust him to let me live once he has what he needs—not when I'd be the only other wolf with the LAG gene. But he's right. I can't exactly refuse him. He'll just take what he wants. He always does. At least, this way, I'll be strong enough to fight back.

Especially now that I'm fighting alone.

"Do we have a deal?" Vincenzo asks.

I take a deep breath and nod. "Deal."

Triumph flashes in his gaze, so vicious it sends a shudder through me. But then he's rising, and the moment changes. The darkness clears. Still, I have the distinct impression I've just negotiated my life away to the devil.

Vincenzo walks over and opens the door. On the other side is a man I've never seen before. For a second, I think he called a doctor after all, but the man simply hands Vincenzo a case then walks away.

Vincenzo closes the door and returns to his seat. He shoves the file aside and sets the case down between us, flicking it open. Then he spins it so I can see what's inside.

A single syringe filled with what looks like blood is nestled in foam.

"What's this?" I ask, fear squeezing my throat so the words come out a little breathless.

"The antidote." When I meet his gaze, he explains, "It's a mixture containing wolf venom. Injecting it will be the same as being bitten except that it'll force the change slowly over the course of a few days rather than all at once."

Trepidation fills me. "You want me to inject this into my body?"

"This is less dangerous than a bite. It contains venom for the change, a gene booster to activate the LAG, and the antidote to the wolfsbane." When I don't respond, his eyes flash with impatience. "Do you want to walk down the aisle with a broken arm?"

Every cell in my body screams at me that this will end badly. If I do this, I can't take it back. Not even if Grey decides to forgive me.

Silence hangs between us for a long moment. Then two. My heartbeat thunders in my ears as I stare at the syringe. It could be a trap. Poison or some other lethal substance. But why go to all this trouble to kill me slowly when he could just shift and rip me apart in seconds?

What he's offering is insanity.

It's also the only thing standing between me and death. The only thing that will provide me protection against these predators. A way to become like Grey. No longer weak. No longer human. A true equal. A mate.

Assuming he still wants me.

With my heart racing, I pick up the syringe and empty its contents into my arm.

29

GREY

I press my foot to the gas, accelerating around the final curve before the familiar turn-off comes into view. Stone pillars mark the address with an iron plate. The massive gate sits open and welcoming—something that would never happen if my father were here. But he's locked up in his Pine Hill fortress. With Lexi.

The drive out to the lake house used to be one of my favorites. Today, I'm too consumed by my own dark thoughts to appreciate it. In my rearview, I catch sight of a familiar SUV trailing me. Honestly, I'm surprised Elio has kept up. My father's keeping close tabs on me, and his loyal little dog hasn't disappointed.

Ignoring him, I flick my gaze back to the road in front of me and narrowly miss clipping the mailbox as I turn in a bit too fast and drive through the open gate. Thick trees obscure the house on my right, offering shade and privacy. Just ahead, a large, detached garage is bordered by evergreens lined with bright pink rhododendrons. I scowl as I remember how much Lexi loved the landscaping out here. This was the first place we found common ground. The place where we agreed to work together.

Did she mean it? Or was she working for Franco even then?

My tires squeal as I come to a stop beside my mother's car. My phone buzzes, and I glance at the incoming call. Dutch. Again. If it's not him, it's Mia.

They all want to know what we're going to do.

I have no fucking idea.

I'm out of moves.

Maybe that's why I'm here instead of back in the city, preparing for my wedding.

Leaving my phone in the car, I climb out and head for the front door. My mother meets me on the porch, dirty gardening gloves clutched in one hand. Her linen pants are a bit smudged with what looks like potting soil, and her cheeks glow with a sun-kissed flush. She looks relaxed, though I suspect that has more to do with her husband being miles away than having her hands in the dirt.

"You made it." She smiles, pulling me into a hug.

I wrap my arms around her, clinging tighter than I have in years. By the time I release her and step back, her forehead is pinched with worry.

"Come in," she says. "We'll sit out back and have some lemonade."

I shake my head. My mother. Approaching life or death with lemonade. "Got anything stronger?" I ask as I follow her inside.

She leads the way through the living room and into the kitchen where memories assault me. This place was my safe haven once. A refuge my mother would escape to when my father became too violent or mean. When I was young, she would bring me with her, and we'd spend weeks here, swimming in the lake or playing board games. Then, I got old enough to be trained in the family business, and my father put his foot down.

She stopped bringing me.

I started accompanying him instead—seeing what he was like with his pack. When she complained that I was becoming too much like him, he blew up. And I saw what he was like with her.

I'm glad she spends so much time here. That she's found somewhere that brings her a shred of peace. But I'm starting to wonder if it's too late for me. Maybe I'm just like my father after all. A monster willing to destroy anyone who gets in his way. Destined for an empty marriage.

"Here." My mom sets a bottle of brandy on the counter.

My brows lift. "That's not exactly strong."

"Well, it's all I've got."

She pulls out an empty glass and heads for the back door. I grab the brandy and follow her outside. A small table and chairs decorate the patio. A pitcher of lemonade and a half-full glass are already sitting on it.

My mother sits, gesturing to the empty chair across from her.

I sit and watch as she pours my cup half-full of lemonade. When she holds it out, I take it but don't bother with the brandy as I drain the contents. For a moment, we sit in silence. I listen to the birds and cicadas, hating how cheerful they sound. Like nature can't be bothered with the fact that my entire world has shattered.

"Do you want to talk about it?" Mom asks.

I bite back a refusal. Talking about it won't change anything, but I can't think of anything else to do. Hell, it's why I drove out here in the first place. So, I shove the words out as quickly as possible. Rip off the Band-Aid.

"Lexi's been spying on me for Franco."

My mother falters then sets her lemonade down. "Are you sure?"

"Yes."

She studies me. "I see. And you're angry."

Temper leaks out, making my words harsher than I intend. "Of course I'm angry. She betrayed me."

"Did she say why?"

I frown. "What?"

"When you asked her about it, did she say why she did it? Was she forced?"

"She's not a wolf who can be compelled." I don't bother to point out that I haven't actually spoken to Lexi about that particular detail. Haven't really spoken to her at all.

"She's a human in a world full of beasts, Grey. She can be threatened—or worse."

I scowl. "I would've protected her. She knows that."

She's silent for a moment, and I can't help feeling defensive at the way she's reacting to this. Like she's on Lexi's side.

"Ramsey admitted he's been doing the same thing," I tell her, needing a reaction that isn't empathy. "He says he's the one who sent those men to the estate last year." Her eyes flash with fear, there and gone quickly. "He almost got you killed."

"Did he say why he did it?" she asks.

"What does it matter?" I snap then take a deep breath. No part of me wants to take this out on her. "He put you in danger. Why didn't you tell me you'd been attacked?"

"Because it wasn't important by the time you came home."

"Your safety's always important to me," I say stubbornly.

"I know, and I love you for it." She softens. "You've always protected everyone else. What about you, darling?"

I glance at my empty lemonade glass, unsure if I can meet her gaze right now. My head swims with so many thoughts—and worries. "I don't know if I can do this," I admit.

"Do what?"

My voice is strained as I say the words I've done my best not to think about. "My wedding's in two days."

She sighs. "I understand. I felt the same way once."

I look up, surprised. "You did?"

"Of course. Just because your father's my mate doesn't mean I ever had any illusions about what kind of man he is."

"I guess I just thought he wasn't always like this."

"He's definitely grown worse over time," she agrees. "But his character's always been the same. His first love will always be himself. And his lack of care for those around him as he pursues what he wants was evident to me even then."

"Why did you marry him then? If you knew who he was?"

"Protection," she says simply. "For you."

My brows lift. "You didn't have me until after you were married."

"No, but I knew my future children were at risk."

I shake my head, confused. "What are you talking about?"

"You know my father worked for GV Industries," she says, and I nod. My grandfather died before I was born, and she rarely talks about him, but I know this much. "His position gave him access to some of Franco's more trusted advisors. During a meeting, he overheard a conversation about how Franco was developing a new drug that would make our wolves more powerful than anything we'd seen before. The executives said the researchers needed test subjects, and when none volunteered, Franco began ordering citizens to participate."

My attention sharpens, and I sit up straighter. "What kind of research?"

She shakes her head. "I don't know details except that he only wanted women of childbearing age. Specifically, women who intended to become pregnant. And only those who were loyal to the Giovanni leadership."

"In other words, Diavolo pack members were excluded."

She nods. "Soon after, my father received a phone call from Franco himself, ordering him to bring his daughter into some clinic to see if I was a viable candidate. By then, I'd already met your father and realized he was my mate. He wasn't the love of my life, but..."

"Marrying him would make you a Diavolo," I realize. "And exempt from testing."

"I did everything I could for you long before you were ever in the picture." She smiles and reaches across the table for my hand, squeezing. "And I don't regret a single thing."

"I appreciate you telling me all of this, Mom. But this isn't the same thing. Lexi's not exactly saving me from a terrible fate."

My mother cocks her head. "Isn't she?" I scowl, refusing to answer that, and she adds, "Without her, you might not have decided to stick around and fight for your own future instead of running away to help others with their wars." My brows lift. How does my mom know so much about my time away? "Seems to me like you're saving each other."

"Does she deserve to be saved?" Even as I ask the question, I can feel the hypocrisy.

Didn't I also scheme with Franco once? And no one forced me. I did it willingly. No matter what Lexi agreed to do, that night, she refused to tell Dom our plans, and he broke her arm. Maybe that was her way of trying to tell me where she stands.

She chose me, and it cost her.

My mother chose my father, and it cost her too.

I sigh, rubbing a hand over my face as my thoughts scatter and reassemble. When I open my eyes, my mother's studying me with a pointed look. "Doesn't everyone deserve a second chance?"

Instead of answering her, I hear myself ask the question that's scarier than any of the ones that came before it. "What if she doesn't want to marry me?"

"Ask her."

"I can't. Dad's locked her up at the estate until the wedding. He won't let me see or talk to her."

She glances toward the side of the house. "Is that why Elio followed you all the way out here?"

"Maybe," I hedge. "Among other reasons."

Her gaze sharpens, and I resist the urge to fidget under her scrutiny. "You feel different," she says quietly.

"What do you mean?"

"You know what I mean. Your wolf calls to me."

Shit.

I knew the alpha in me was growing stronger, but I didn't realize others could sense it yet. Not like this. That means I'm dangerously close to outing myself even without using the hex blade to form the pack.

Still, I don't bother to deny what she's implying. "Marrying Lexi means staying to deal with everything," I say instead.

She nods, understanding what I don't want to say out loud. That it means facing off with my father—and only one of us walking away. She leans forward, her expression vulnerable and earnest. With watery eyes, she whispers, "I'm proud of you."

My throat tightens. "Thanks, Mom."

We share a moment of silence that's full of years' worth of unspoken alliances. All the times she wanted to protect me. All the moments I wished I could save her. Then she blinks and sits back, her expression clearing.

"Look, I can't tell you what to do about Lexi, but I think some things you have to take on faith," she says. "What does your heart tell you?"

I exhale. "That Lexi's it for me. No matter what."

"Then that's all you need to know."

"Mom, there are a million factors here. Dad—"

"Trust fate, sweetie. It brought her to you. It won't let you down."

I shake my head. At this point, I'm not sure fate deserves that kind of trust, considering everything else it's dealt me. Or her. But I don't have the heart to argue with her. "Thanks, Mom. I appreciate this."

"Of course. Now get going. You have a wedding to prepare for."

I manage an almost-smile as she hugs me goodbye and shoos me out the door again. Elio watches me from inside his SUV. Just to piss him off, I smile at him and wave, all the while imagining him driving straight off a cliff on the way home.

Maybe fate can start there.

My phone's already buzzing when I open my car door and climb inside. With renewed determination, I pick it up and answer it. "Hey, Dutch. What's up?"

"Dude, where the fuck have you been?" Dutch's tone is more urgent and exasperated than I expect—even for ghosting him all day.

"Is that him?" Mia's voice in the background is nearly a shriek. "Put him on speaker."

"What the hell's going on?" I demand.

"We've been trying to call you." I hear shuffling, and when Dutch speaks again, his voice echoes, letting me know I'm on speaker now. "It's Ramsey."

My good mood vanishes. "What about him?"

Mia snarls, "He escaped."

30

LEXI

Grey doesn't come to see me. Or if he does, Vincenzo doesn't let him in. I try pressing my ear to the front door of my little apartment-prison to eavesdrop, but I can't hear anything beyond the shuffling of guards as they pace outside my door. Eventually, I give up. For the rest of the evening, I watch movies to distract myself, but I can't stop wondering whether Grey's absence is an indication of what's to come.

I'd hoped he'd at least let me explain myself, but what if he's already made up his mind? The fear and hurt eat away at me, gnawing a hole through what's left of my heart.

My only visitor is a guard who delivers my dinner: a greasy bag of fast food that's already cold. When I try to request a meeting with Vincenzo, the guard snaps at me to go back inside and practically shoves me so he can pull the door shut in my face. I eat, knowing I need my strength for whatever comes next, and try not to think about what horrible future awaits me now that I've made my deal with Vincenzo.

My arm aches at the injection site, though not nearly as badly as the broken bone that's begun to swell and pulse. I'm not sure if it's smart to hope the serum works. I'd be stronger then. A wolf—capable of fighting off my enemies. Maybe even stronger than all of them. But I'd also have to hand over the very thing that makes me so powerful—to the one man who won't hesitate to use it against us all.

Will Grey forgive me for that too?

Eventually, I fall asleep, only to dream of a wedding where everyone else shows up as a wolf, and Vincenzo rips their throats out right in front of me until I'm alone in a cathedral of blood and bones.

The next day, when I open the door to the guard bringing me food, I hear yelling and glass breaking coming from inside the main house. I wince, but the guard's expression remains unchanged. He either has the best poker face ever, or he's used to this kind of chaos.

"What's happening?" I ask.

"Nothing. Eat."

I scowl at him and close the door.

An hour later, there's another knock. Hope and anticipation have me hurrying to answer it. Grey. It has to be him. But I open the door to Charlie Reyes instead. Behind him, the house is quiet, but his expression isn't quite as smooth as the guard's was.

"Can I come in?" he asks.

"Sure." I pull the door open to let him pass then close it behind him with a soft click.

He paces into the living room then turns around to face me. There are dark circles beneath his eyes, but it's the pinched shape of his mouth that sets me on edge. The fact that he's willing to show me his worry—or is too stressed to hide it—tightens my stomach.

"What's wrong?" I ask.

His gaze flicks to my injured arm, which is a lot less swollen today. And a lot less painful. "Did you know Ramsey was informing to Franco?"

I blink, fear spreading through me like poison. "What?"

"No, of course you didn't. You barely know him." He shakes his head and goes back to pacing.

Suddenly, the destruction I heard earlier makes sense. Vincenzo must be losing his mind, knowing he's had a traitor in his midst. Then my stomach turns to lead as Grey's lack of communication hits me. If Ramsey's been discovered, there's no telling what he said about me to save himself.

"Wow." I force myself to sound shocked. "How did he find out something like that? Did Ramsey confess?"

"Not exactly. Apparently, Grey found out he'd been informing and locked him in one of our abandoned warehouses for questioning. Ramsey escaped yesterday and was picked up by one of our men leaving Altobello's late last night. He's in our custody now."

Altobello's. That's Franco's restaurant.

Fear grips my heart, squeezing until my breath catches. I swallow hard, forcing myself to sound as unaffected as possible, but my voice comes out way too strained. "Has Ramsey said anything else? About his dealings with Franco, I mean?"

He studies me, his lips pressed together in a tight line like he's judging whether I can handle more. "Nothing yet. But I'm sure it's only a matter of time." He grimaces. "We won't go easy on him."

All the air rushes from my lungs. Whatever Vincenzo's men are doing to Ramsey now, they'll do the same to me once they find out I'm part of it.

The oxygen in the room is suddenly too thin. I wheeze, gripping the side of the couch for support.

"Are you all right?" Charlie asks, and I look up to see him frowning at me.

Straightening, I smooth my expression, forcing what I hope is a smile. "I'm fine. It's just a lot to take in. Ramsey's put everyone at risk."

His expression is sympathetic. "Grey really is your mate then."

I blow out a shaky breath. There's no point in lying. Not about this. "Yes."

He shoves his hands into his pockets, and for a moment, he looks less like a mafia general than I've ever seen him. "Can I give you some advice?" he asks quietly.

His tone is the same one he used on the balcony when he dropped the drunk act to tell me about that file.

"Sure."

"Don't trust Vincenzo or that serum he's offering. It's not worth it. And it's not what you think."

"What do you mean?" I ask, my blood chilling.

"Your wolf isn't worth being controlled by someone like him. Find another way."

"How would he control my wolf—?"

Someone knocks, and the door's shoved open. A guard pokes his head in. "Boss is asking for you," he tells Charlie.

"I'm coming." Charlie takes his hands out of his pockets, his expression hardening as if he's donning a mask.

He starts for the door, the guard pushing it wide to give him room. I bite my tongue as he leaves, knowing better than to expect more answers from someone who just risked his own life to give me the warning in the first place.

When he's gone, I sink to the floor and stare at the twist tie around my finger, wondering if it means anything at all. Or if I'll even live long enough to find out.

31

GREY

It takes me longer than I'd like to get back to the city and longer still to lose Elio in traffic. Dutch, Mia, Razor, and Crow are all waiting at the warehouse when I finally arrive. From the looks of it, Razor's nose is broken, but otherwise, he seems fine. The rest of them are red-faced and tense.

"What happened?" I ask, walking up to where they wait by the door.

"He pretended his leg was broken," Razor says. He's holding a bloodied rag, and his nose is crusted with dried blood. "After that last round I went on him, I thought it was. So, I untied his ankles so he could piss with some dignity. Ugh, dammit, I'm such a fucking idiot."

"This isn't on you," Dutch says, but he and I share a look.

This won't remain contained. Not with Ramsey out there saying who knows what.

"What do you want to do?" Mia asks.

Her tone is sharp, her gaze piercing. She's shaken—more than usual. And Mia doesn't rile easily. Guilt twists inside me. I fucked this up by going after Dom. Otherwise, I could've challenged my father and been alpha right now. We'd have one less threat at our backs. Instead, we have to worry about how guilty we all look. Because I already know Ramsey's betrayal will affect us all. If Franco doesn't come after us, my father will. He'll never believe Ramsey acted alone. Not with how close we've all been.

"Should we go look for him?" Razor's tone borders on panic.

"No. We're going to my house," I say quietly.

"For what?" Crow looks wary. Like he can't decide between wanting to fight and knowing it's futile.

I can't blame him.

But I refuse to give up. Five years ago, my plan failed, but that's not the part I regret. When it was over, I left—licked my wounds and convinced myself I didn't owe anything to anyone, including myself.

I won't walk away again.

This time, I'm all in.

"The hex blade," I say. "It's time we took the oath and became a real pack."

"Your father will know," Mia warns.

"It's the only way we'll be strong enough when he comes for us," I tell them. "But the choice is yours. You don't have to do this. There's no going back if you do."

"Hell yeah, we're doing this," Razor says fervently.

"It's not just my old man coming this time," I warn him. "All the generals will back him. He won't fight fair. You ready for that?"

Razor glances at Crow, his jaw set. "It's past time they paid for their sins."

I nod and look at the others.

"You know I'm in," Dutch says.

"You're the only family I have," Crow says, eyes glittering with a quiet resolve. "I will always choose you guys."

We all turn to Mia.

Her expression is strained. She, more than any of us, undoubtedly feels the conflict of this decision. Her dad's been the most decent of any of ours. Forming a pack with us means walking away from any allegiance she has to him.

Crow speaks up first. "Mia, we understand if you—"

"Yeah, obviously I'm in," she says quickly. He smiles, and she bumps her shoulder with his. "Someone has to keep you assholes in line."

Dutch grins at Crow.

Razor hoots.

"Okay," I say, my alpha already stirring. The transition is nearly complete now. All that's left is their pledge in blood. "Let's go become a pack."

~

I open my eyes and sit up, blinking so that my sight adjusts quickly to the shadows of my bedroom. It's not a sound that wakes me; it's the silence. Or maybe it's the knowing—a sudden sensation stemming from the beast inside me that tells me I'm not alone. That power has joined me in this room. A lone figure stands at the foot of my bed.

I recognize him with a jolt of awareness—and fear.

"Franco," I say quietly. "To what do I owe this surprise?"

"We need to talk." He doesn't wait for my answer before turning and walking out. A moment later, I can hear the clink of glass. Helping himself to my wet bar.

I check my phone; it's three in the morning.

Shit.

Bracing myself for whatever this is, I toss back the covers in search of clothing. When I've pulled on sweatpants and a tee, I make my way out to the living room.

Dressed in a suit, Franco sits with his legs crossed in Dutch's favorite chair. He holds a shot of whiskey in his hand. A quick sweep of the space reveals he's here alone. Not that I think he's stupid enough to have left his men at home. Probably waiting for his signal to swoop in and kill me.

Then again, he's the high alpha of the mafia pack. He doesn't need backup to take me out.

"What can I do for you?" I ask.

"You were smart to send the rat," he says. "I'd suspect manipulation less from someone simple-minded like him, but I know you better than you think."

Ramsey. I keep my face carefully blank and take a seat. My posture is casual, careless; my thoughts are anything but. "We discovered Ramsey was an informant. We tried to apprehend him, but he managed to slip away. If you know where he is, I'd appreciate that information."

"He came to see me. Tried to tell me some story about how you'd decided to leave town again. Said there would be no wedding so not to bother showing up. When I scented his lies, I sent him on his pathetic way."

Ramsey told him the wedding was off?

"I have no control over what he says to you or anyone else."

Franco's expression tightens. It's almost like a smile but so much worse. "Do you want to know why I allowed you to take on that fight five years ago?"

I don't answer, but he doesn't seem to need me to.

"Your father was made a general because he's just like Ramsey. Power-hungry, ruthless—and simple. Vincenzo's strategies are predictable and his methods rudimentary. He'll never be a match for me. It's the reason I've allowed him to live this long even while he stirs divisiveness among the packs." He swirls his glass, staring into it. "Tio was the same. So was Dom. So have they all been." His gaze lifts to mine. "Except for you."

His words might sound like a compliment, but I know better. I keep my expression carefully neutral.

"You were always the greater threat, Jericho. Dom knew it at the end."

Shit.

This is why he's here.

He knows.

"I'm not sure what you—"

"Don't bullshit me," he snaps, voice rising. "You took my second from me. And tried to use the rat to paint a target on your father. You don't think I see through your strategy? You don't think I know you want me to do your dirty work for you?"

My heart pounds, my thoughts racing as I try to make sense of his words. Ramsey told him it was my father? Was he trying to help us? To redeem himself? Where is he now?

"My father plans to kill you," I say. "That's not a manipulation, that's a fact."

"Your father's a blunt instrument."

Frustration threatens my control. "What's the super-alpha gene?"

His eyes widen fractionally, and I know I've struck gold. "Nothing," he mutters, turning to his glass and taking a thoughtful sip.

"Dom was going to kill Lexi over it. That's why I put him down."

His gaze snaps back to mine, his eyes narrowing. His alpha power rises, the pressure of it pushing me back into my seat. "What do you know about the gene?" he demands.

Sweat dots my brow as I work to resist his compulsion. "I know you're embezzling money from the city budget—including stealing from public schools—in order to fund your research."

His eyes widen. "Does Vincenzo know about this?"

"He's been speaking to a doctor from your past," I say. "I don't know what he knows."

He snarls, clearly pissed off, but he doesn't press me for anything else. A second later, he exhales, his entire body sagging, and the power that had pinned me recedes. I suck in a deep breath that feels lighter and easier to draw than it did a moment ago.

Franco hangs his head, winded and exhausted.

I've never seen him look so drained before.

"What will happen if Lexi is bitten?" I ask.

He looks up at me, his mouth sagging and deep lines etched around his eyes. He looks as if he's just aged thirty years, and when he speaks, his answer is devoid of caring. "She'll die."

Anger surges to the surface, too hot and fast for me to care that it might be reckless to unleash it. "Tell me how to keep her alive."

"Watch how you speak to me," he snaps, but the power that rushes at his words is only a fraction of what it was earlier.

"She's your own blood," I say, refusing to let it go. "Why doesn't that matter to you?"

"It mattered more than you know," he says sadly.

"Is that why you experimented on her?" My voice twists angrily, but rather than raising his temper, he looks surprised. "Did you think your secrets were buried, old man?"

He shakes his head. "Buried or not, we failed."

"What did you do to her?"

"I tried to make her strong, to make her powerful."

"Why?" I demand.

He doesn't answer, but the silence speaks volumes.

"You wanted it for yourself," I realize. "She was just the guinea pig."

"She would've made history," he snaps. "Do you know what it's like to be the strongest alpha this pack has ever seen—and then feel it slowly draining away from you? To know your days are numbered. That one day, your strength will fail, and you'll lose everything you've built?" His chest rises and falls with heavy breaths. "Those tests were about finding a way to prolong my leadership."

"Is that what you told the women you experimented on?" I demand. "Is that what you told Carina? What you would've told my mother?"

His expression hardens. "I did what I did for the good of the pack. Otherwise, we risk a man like your father leading."

My hands ball into fists at the way he talks about using people with such disregard. "You did it for you. No one else, old man."

Anger flashes in his eyes. He moves to the edge of his chair, his drink sloshing in his hand. "You want to keep Lexi out of your father's control? I'll tell you what. Tomorrow, I'll go to your wedding just like Vincenzo wants—and I'll bite her myself."

He pushes to his feet at the same time I do.

"No!" I roar. "You will not touch her."

He tilts his head, his power poking and prodding at

mine. Then his eyes widen. "She's your mate." There's shock and awe in his voice, but just as quickly as it comes, it's replaced with regret. "If only it were enough."

Then he walks back to the bar where he shoves his glass of whiskey.

"Bite her yourself then. She'll either shift, or she'll die. If she shifts, she might be worthy of whatever challenge your father issues against her. If she dies, she was never good enough to be my heir in the first place."

"Did Lexi agree to spy for you willingly?"

He glances over before waving his hand at me dismissively. "Bah. She won't live long enough for it to matter now, will she?"

He starts for the door, and the sight of him walking away from me unleashes everything I've so tightly locked away.

My wolf surges to the surface—as does the full force of the alpha power I've possessed since the moment my pack pledged themselves to me.

A power that's grown stronger in the shadows where I've nursed it.

Now, I let it free.

"We're done when I say we're done," I boom.

The pressure pins him, stooping his back and shoulders until his knees begin to buckle. With labored breaths, he manages to look up at me with wide eyes. "I don't fucking believe it," he manages. "You're an alpha." Rage contorts his expression. "But you won't be for much longer."

He trembles as his wolf rises to the surface. Murder

swims in his gaze. A thirst for blood that fills my veins too.

With a roar, I shift, leaping over the couch as bones break and fur sprouts. My canines shove through my gums. My claws rip at the carpet beneath my feet.

Franco's power rushes to meet mine then drains away.

"No," he manages weakly.

But I'm done taking orders from the alphas of this pack.

My teeth sink into his shoulder. It's not a fatal blow, but I rip through flesh and sinew anyway, tearing a hole in the monster himself. He screams, and I brace myself for his men to come running.

A second bite has him thrashing, his body contorting as he tries to shift and fight me off. I shove at him with my paw, letting him turn onto his back. His human body becomes a wolf just as I sink my teeth into his throat. His claws sprout, burying themselves in my belly. The pain registers somewhere I can't be reached.

His blood and tissue fill my mouth.

His alpha power hits me like a bolt of lightning, nearly breaking my hold on his neck. The wind is knocked from me as the power presses down around me like a weight.

Stop.

His alpha command is a mindfuck. So much worse than anything my father's capable of. My teeth begin to loosen their grip. Before my jaw can unhinge, I yank, ripping his throat out just like I did to Dom.

When I'm done, I climb off him and stand over his lifeless wolf, sprawled and bloody where he lies on my floor.

Rivers of blood pour from his torn throat, pooling and spreading over the pristine carpet.

I heave in breath after breath, tasting copper.

Shock keeps me rooted to the spot. Or maybe it's the last dregs of his alpha command. Eventually, it fades, along with his life, and the weight lifts.

My autonomy returns.

The alpha inside me expands with its newfound power. The life force of a high alpha is no small thing. Whatever Franco had left in him, it's mine now.

The mafia pack is mine too.

I don't move for another long moment as the truth of that sinks in. When I finally do, I back away, shifting to my human form as I hurry for the elevator keypad. With the press of a button, I lock it down. No one in or out without my access code. Then, I rush back to the phone I left on my nightstand and open my security app.

A quick scan of the cameras surrounding the exits yields nothing.

Franco really came here alone.

Was he insane?

No, just arrogant.

He really thought he'd walk out of here. Hell, so did I.

And now, he won't. And the world will know.

My thoughts race ahead to tomorrow. Consequences, inevitable scenarios—I know how this ends. Franco's empire belongs to me now, but only if I can keep it. And Franco's generals will never allow that. My father will never allow that. They'll come for me—and even with all this newfound power, I'm not sure our fledgling pack can withstand a war on two fronts.

I was supposed to earn the loyalty of my father's pack first. Get more of them to fight on our side when the time came to face Franco. Challenging and beating my father would've done that. I'm his son. His pack already sees me as their next alpha.

But I've just taken the kingdom of my enemy. Franco's pack will never accept me. His generals will never pledge to me.

There's only one person they might accept.

Shaking, I pull up my contacts and call Dutch.

He answers, groggy. "Boss?"

"I need you to come over. Alone. Don't say a word to anyone, and don't be seen by any of the cameras. Do you understand?"

"You okay? You sound…different."

I swallow the power that's been rooting inside me from the moment Franco's heart stopped beating.

"All good," I lie. "Just get here soon. We have work to do."

32

LEXI

With a pounding heart, I peer through the small opening in the stained-glass window that overlooks the sanctuary below. The church is packed. I'm not sure who invited all these people or even who they are, but it feels as if everyone in Indigo Hills has turned up for what the newspaper sitting on my dressing table has dubbed the "Cinderella Wedding." It's the biggest line of bullshit they could've chosen. I'm not a princess, no matter how many times they call me that, and no matter how much I want it to, I'm pretty sure this story has no happy ending for me.

Even if I'm dressed like a queen.

Slowly, I peel myself away from the sight of the crowd and return to the mirror where I confront a stranger.

Three hours ago, Vincenzo's guards delivered me to this small second-floor room inside the same church where Anthony's funeral was held just days ago and locked me inside. A heavy garment bag was already here waiting for me when I arrived. Inside, I found a beautiful white dress that fit as perfectly as if it were made for my body.

Hell, maybe it was.

This town, and Vincenzo's role in it, thrives on appearances, so I'm not surprised he spared no expense on my wedding dress. Putting it on felt like tempting fate.

I still haven't spoken to Grey.

Just thinking about him makes my heart squeeze and my eyes prick. I have no idea what he's going to do today. Will he show up? Will he say the vows?

After the secret I kept, I can't blame him if he decides to walk away. Start over. Just like he did five years ago.

After what I've done, I can't expect him to love me. To save me.

Grey was never supposed to be my knight in shining armor anyway. He's the kind of man who puts you in danger before getting you out of it again. I have zero illusions about who and what he is, but that hasn't stopped my feelings for him. Somewhere along the way, I went and fell for the villain. The kind of man who sees someone hurting me and rips out his throat without hesitation. I don't know what kind of monster it makes me, but he's exactly the kind of man I want to marry.

I just hope he'll forgive everything I've done to get here.

Not just the agreement I made with Franco but the one I made with his father.

I'm still not sure when the full change will hit me. But

the venom's already healed my arm and heightened my senses—which only makes my fear worse.

I have no idea how long I sit like this, but eventually, someone knocks.

I scramble back just as the door's unlocked and shoved open.

An armed guard peers down at me, frowning. "You have two minutes." I don't answer, and he starts to shut the door before opening it again and adding, "Might want to fix your makeup."

He shuts the door just as I lift my middle finger at him.

Two minutes.

The silence hits me then, and I find myself wishing Violet were here. Or Mia. Someone to say encouraging things that have nothing to do with wars and wolves. To make me feel like I'm just a girl about to walk down the aisle.

But like everything else in my life, I'll have to do this alone.

Careful not to step on my dress, I climb to my feet and walk into the tiny, attached bathroom. Sure enough, mascara has run onto my cheeks in thick, black lines. I wash my face and stare at my reflection, noting my red-rimmed eyes and flushed cheeks.

The door opens again.

"It's time," the guard snaps.

Hurrying, I reapply lip gloss and abandon the rest. It'll have to be enough.

He waves me out first, and with a fistful of my dress clutched in one hand and my bouquet in the other, I carefully descend the stairs. When I reach the bottom, I falter.

My insides twist as a sharp pain pierces all the way through to my bones. I've had other twinges since injecting myself, but not like this. Pure fire burns through me for a long moment.

I gasp, clutching my abdomen.

The guard comes up behind me and nudges me impatiently. "Get moving. The music's started."

Just as suddenly as it came, the pain vanishes, and I look up, my senses suddenly returning with a whoosh.

He's right.

The organ's playing the wedding march. Inside the sanctuary, everyone is already standing.

It's my cue.

Forcing myself to breathe deeply, I adjust my dress and smooth it with clammy palms before starting forward. A few short steps later, I emerge into the crowded sanctuary then stop again, overwhelmed by the weight of this moment. Every head turns to watch me. But their faces are a blur as I sweep my gaze past them and down the long aisle to the front.

The sight of Grey standing there in a dark suit threatens to bring me to my knees.

He's here.

At the altar.

His eyes find mine, and I stop breathing.

The organ pauses on the last note of its song then starts again, this time louder—with emphasis for the bride to get her ass in gear, no doubt.

I start walking.

With shaky hands, I grip my bouquet and try not to trip.

Murmurs hum as I pass, comments I don't bother to tune in to. Whatever they're saying, it's not for my ears. The only thing I care about is the man waiting for me at the altar.

So I keep my eyes locked on him and put one foot in front of the other.

When I finally reach the dais, he holds out a hand, and I take it, stepping up until we're standing side by side. He turns to face me, and a thousand emotions rise inside me as my gaze fastens on his. The crowd disappears. Everything else falls away. There's only him.

His dark, depthless eyes that silently promise to protect me no matter what. The fullness of a mouth so readily capable of making me forget everything but his kiss. Arms that have held me, fought for me. Shoulders I've cried on. And his beautiful tattoos peeking out from beneath his cuffs.

My heightened senses drink him in like I'm seeing him for the first time.

Relief slams into me so hard my throat constricts with the effort not to burst into tears.

"You look so beautiful," he says, his voice full of wonder.

I attempt a watery smile. "You do too."

His lips twitch. At the direction of the priest, he takes both my hands in his and holds them tightly. His touch sends a shudder through me like my senses are on overload.

Grey's eyes narrow in concern. "Are you okay?" he whispers.

"I'm not sure," I admit, wishing there'd been time to explain what I've done. The serum. My bargain with Vincenzo. He won't like it. But I made my decision, and there's no going back now.

"Everything's going to be okay," he murmurs. His lips quirk up in a secret smile that feels more reassuring than I could've expected. Like he knows something. Or has done something.

Like everything really will be okay.

"Your father—" I begin, darting a look at the faces in the front row. I glimpse only Mia and Razor before his next words call me back.

"Isn't a threat to us anymore," he whispers, eyes gleaming with confidence.

The priest clears his throat.

Grey ignores him, all his attention on me. Like we're the only ones in this crowded church. He lifts our joined hands and brushes a kiss over my knuckles. "I'm sorry I didn't tell you we're mates," he says quietly. "Can you forgive me?"

"Yes," I whisper. "Can you forgive me?"

"I know what happened, and there's nothing to forgive. Now, all I want is for you to know that this is real for me."

My heart swells. Hope turns to something more. Elation, exhilaration, love. "It's real for me too," I whisper back.

He grins, his entire face lighting up.

We turn to the priest, who watches us with raised brows. "Are we ready now?"

"We're ready," Grey and I say in unison.

He squeezes my hand as the priest begins to speak to the crowd.

I squeeze it back.

Maybe it's a Cinderella wedding after all.

33

GREY

The vows are short and sweet, but I don't mind that. I say them with every ounce of conviction inside me. When the priest asks if there's anything I want to add, I look right into Lexi's eyes and tell her how I feel.

"You are my world, my first and last breath, the reason for my heartbeat, Lexi Ryall." She smirks at the use of her human last name. The one she insisted I call her because she refused to be lumped in with Franco. "I can't promise to be perfect, but I swear to honor and protect you with everything I am. And I promise to love you with every single cell of my body—wolf and man—for as long as I live."

Lexi's eyes glimmer with tears.

Then, I listen as Lexi repeats her vows to me, her voice wobbly with emotion.

"Is there anything you'd like to add?" the priest asks her.

She takes a deep breath. "Jericho Grey Diavolo, I didn't exactly see you coming—which you made sure of." Someone in the front row snickers. "And honestly, at first, I couldn't wait to get away from you. But even before we were friends, you protected me. Then you gave me roots. Somewhere and someone to belong to. I've never had that before. And now that I do, I don't plan to ever give it up. I love you."

When it's time for the rings to be exchanged, I slide a simple wedding band onto her finger alongside the diamond. My eyes catch on the twist tie still tucked beneath her engagement ring. Then she holds a matching one up for me and, with a laugh, I let her wrap it around my ring finger.

We share a smile, and hers is so luminous, proud, and full of love that it stops my heart.

The priest says something, but I'm too busy kissing Lexi to hear him. She makes a sound of surprise, but it's quickly drowned out by a voice that suddenly yells, "Wait! Stop! Alpha down!"

Fuck.

I'd been so caught up in Lexi's words and the wonder of knowing she meant them I'd almost forgotten the plan.

Heart racing, I break the kiss, holding Lexi's arms firmly as Dutch comes running down the aisle. The guests are stunned, but my father's men are already closing in on him. They weren't permitted their guns inside the church, which is a relief. Otherwise, there's a good chance Dutch wouldn't have made it this far.

"Alpha down," Dutch repeats, his expression shocked.

My father stands up. "What the hell's going on?"

"It's Franco…" Dutch trails off, clearly winded. His face is flushed. He looks confused and more than a little disturbed.

On the other side of the aisle, Santiago pushes to his feet alongside Conrad and Toros.

"What about the alpha?" Santiago demands.

Dutch looks at the general with wide eyes and says, "He's dead."

The crowd offers a collective gasp.

I stare at Dutch, my eyes boring holes into my friend, willing him to finish it.

Before the crowd can drown him out, he points at Lexi. "The alpha's body is in her room. His throat's been torn out. I can't scent anyone inside that room but her." He pauses to catch his breath before adding, "She killed him." He points at Lexi as he declares, "By pack law, Lexi Giovanni is declared high alpha of the Mafia Wolf Pack."

The crowd is silent for a full weighted breath—and then they erupt into chaos.

I look over at Lexi, bracing myself for shock, or surprise, or even panic. Her eyes, a beautiful dark green, flash golden amber, narrowing to slits like a predator's. Then she blinks, and the change is gone.

Confusion roots me where I stand. Scanning her, I search for some sign that she's been bitten. But her skin remains unbroken.

The wolf inside her surges.

I feel it as certainly as I can feel my own.

My gaze catches on her arm. Two days ago, it was broken. Now, it moves with ease.

Healed.

There's only one thing that could've done that.

Horror spreads through me, inky black and heavier than any alpha power. Her gaze meets mine with the same alarm I feel.

In unison, we say to each other, "What have you done?"

Find out what happens next in Broken Wolf Heart!

Get a special bonus scene from Deadly Wolf Bite!
Visit bit.ly/DeadlyBonus

Want more from this world?

Check out The Lone Wolf Pack series & The Black Moon Pack series for interconnected shifter romance stories and see which characters from the Mafia Pack make an appearance.

Find out more including series reading order at https://www.heatherhildenbrand.com/series-reading-order.

BROKEN WOLF HEART

In a city full of wolf shifters willing to kill for their own gain, I found a man who would die to protect me.

My mate is no Prince Charming.

If anything, he's the villain.

Willing to do anything for the people he loves.

I'm no different.

I made a deal with the devil to become a beast.

And now, just when I've glimpsed happiness, that deal will cost me everything.

Maybe even my mate.

In the midst of murder and chaos, I've become a queen of wolves. But what good is a crown with no king to share it?

Get Book 3, Broken Wolf Heart!

ABOUT THE AUTHOR

Heather Hildenbrand lives in coastal Virginia where she writes paranormal and fantasy romance with lots of kissing & killing. Her most frequent hobbies are cuddling with her 100-pound goldendoodle, riding country roads on the back of her husband's motorcycle, and avoiding killer slugs.

You can find out more about Heather and her books at www.heatherhildenbrand.com.

Or find her here:

TikTok
Patreon
Facebook group
Instagram

ALSO BY HEATHER HILDENBRAND

One Dark Spark

Two Blazing Hearts

Three Scorched Kingdoms

Dark Wolf Soul

Deadly Wolf Bite

Broken Wolf Heart

Kingdom of Briars and Roses (Cursed Fae)

Protect Me (Immortal Vices & Virtues)

Hunt Me (Immortal Vices & Virtues)

Consume Me (Immortal Vices & Virtues)

To Hunt A Wolf

To Kiss A Wolf

To Keep A Wolf

Midnight Cursed

Midnight Hunted

Midnight Bound

Wolf Cursed

Wolf Captive

Wolf Chosen

Wolf Revealed

A Witch's Call

A Witch's Destiny

A Witch's Fate

A Witch's Soul

A Witch's Prophecy

A Witch's Hope

Twisted Tides

The Girl Who Cried Werewolf

The Girl Who Cried Captive

The Girl Who Cried War

The Girl Who Never Cried

The Winter Witch

The Spring Witch

The Witch's Heart

Midnight Mate

Goddess Ascending

Goddess Claiming

Goddess Forging

Kiss of Death

Knock Em Dead

Death's Door

Dead to Rights

Dead End

The Girl Who Called The Stars

The Girl Who Ruled The Stars

Alpha Games

Alpha Trials

Alpha Chosen

Dirty Blood

Cold Blood

Blood Bond

Blood Rule

Broken Blood

Imitation

Deviation

Generation

Heather also writes small-town contemporary romance as Violet Stafford.

Stay For Summer

The Breakup Bet

www.ingramcontent.com/pod-product-compliance
Lightning Source LLC
Chambersburg PA
CBHW020338310726
48979CB00015B/2420/J

9781961455252